There wasn't any reason Maggie could see for leaving the comfortable, big town house in the middle of night, and traveling over bumpy roads until morning. Presumably Miss Dolly, romantic and sad-eyed Miss Dolly, knew what she was doing. But when their destination came in sight, Maggie was more certain than ever that the whole thing was a mistake. A ramshackle and rather dirty cottage by a lake—that is what they had taken such pains and insisted on such secrecy to reach. There were only two young men in it, of whom Maggie instantly disapproved, and no one else around—until the lawyer appeared. But then, he was only there so short a time. . . .

Mrs. Holding's talent for creating endearing and completely credible heroines, who manage to involve themselves in really sinister situations, has never been more admirably demonstrated than it is here.

I0629059

KILL JOY

by

ELISABETH SANXAY HOLDING

WILDSIDE PRESS

KILL JOY

ONE

I T WAS NEARLY half-past two when Mrs. Crabtree and Maggie had finished their lunch and the last of the dishes was dried and put away.

"Are you coming upstairs now, Mrs. Crabtree?" Maggie asked.

"No," said Mrs. Crabtree. "No, Maggie, I think I'll stop here a bit and read my paper."

That was bad news for Maggie. Mr. Camford was home this afternoon, and she dreaded the prospect of meeting him alone in the hall. She hated his way of looking at her, an annoyed and embarrassed way, as if she were an intruder from another world. As if she were a servant, a mere servant. And she was not. She might be employed here as a maid; but that was of no significance, it was only temporary. She was a high school graduate, and a very proud girl.

"No," Mrs. Crabtree said again, "I want to read about this murder."

"Oh, Mrs. Amber?" said Maggie. "That's a terrible thing, isn't it?"

"Well," said Mrs. Crabtree, "she brought it on herself."

"Oh, d'you think so?" asked Maggie.

"They all do," said Mrs. Crabtree, settling herself in her rocking-chair with a comfortable creaking.

She was an Englishwoman of great dignity and composure, stout, high-waisted, with grey hair crimped and parted in the middle; when she put on her spectacles, she had the benign authority of a fairy godmother.

"Well, but how?" asked Maggie.

"These women that get themselves murdered . . ." said Mrs. Crabtree. "When you study the cases like I do, you'll

5

see how they've all been flouncing around in these pajamas and these shorts—and shorts they are. They all get themselves mixed up with men, one way or another."

"But *anybody* could get murdered," said Maggie.

"They could," said Mrs. Crabtree. "But they don't. They bring it on themselves."

"Well, I've read about girls, respectable girls—" said Maggie, resisting this new theory.

"Yes, said Mrs. Crabtree, "but study the cases, and you'll see they've done something very foolish like going down in a cellar with one of these foreigners, or taking a ride with a gunman. You'd better go up and change now, Maggie. It's getting on, and Mrs. Mayfield likes you to be ready in your black uniform by three o'clock."

It was hard to leave the neat tranquil kitchen and the company of the admirable Mrs. Crabtree. But it was Maggie's duty to go, and she always did her duty. Always. She went up the dark flight of stairs from the basement, and that was all right, these stairs belonged to Mrs. Crabtree and herself. But there were no back stairs in this house, and when she reached the top of this flight, she was in Mr. Camford's domain.

He might be right there in the sitting-room, she thought, and she wanted to run, she felt limp and bedraggled in her blue cotton dress. But she would not run, she walked straight as an arrow, a pretty little thing with vivid blue eyes and crisp coppery hair and a creamy skin dusted with tiny freckles.

I don't care, she told herself. I'm doing the job I'm paid to do, that's all. This is a democratic country. I don't have to stay—like this. Some day, who knows? I might meet Mr. Camford at a party some day, when I'm a private secretary, or married to somebody much better than *he* is.

She got safely past the sitting-room and mounted the second flight, and there in the hall she nearly ran into Mr. Camford coming out of the bathroom. He was in his dressing-gown, too, which made it worse. He stepped aside, and so did she, so that they still faced each other; he raised his eyebrows, a tall, lean, bald man, ineffably distinguished. Maggie stepped to one side again, and so did he, and there they still were.

He made a faint tut-tut sound and turned away, back toward the bathroom, as if he could not endure the sight of her, and she went on toward the last flight, her cheeks burn-

6

ing, a hot resentment in her heart. He's *mean*, she said to herself. He could speak, couldn't he? Or even smile. You'd think I was—I don't know what. Dirt beneath his feet. All right! One of these days, I'll show him, the mean old thing.

She went into her own small room and closed the door, she went to the chest of drawers, and leaning her elbows on it, looked at the picture of her mother which stood there in a leather frame, a sandy-haired little woman with a thin, fine face. Her mother's idea, this had been. You could get a nice place with a private family, she had said. You mean, be a *servant?* her daughter had demanded. Yes, Mrs. MacGowan had said. You'd learn more about life in that way than ever you could in an office, and when you come to figure it out, you get more money.

Maggie had utterly repudiated that suggestion. She had decided to get a nice job in an office, and why not? She had taken a commercial course in high school, and she had done well in it, as in all her studies; she had a good opinion of her abilities. The reception she got at employment agencies surprised and displeased her. It was undeniable that she had had no experience, but she sat and talked to other girls just out of business school who were sent out to get jobs. She had some interviews, but nothing came of them.

"I don't see why it is that I don't get a job," she said to another girl waiting in an agency.

"Well," said this other girl with impersonal candor, "I think it's because you're kind of old-fashioned." "Old-fashioned?" Maggie repeated. "Yes, kind of," this other girl said. "There's nothing old-fashioned about *me*," Maggie said briefly.

But on the way home, she looked critically at herself in shop windows, and doubts assailed her, to see that straight small figure in a long grey coat and a round felt hat . . . There was only one week left. Mrs. MacGowan was going off to Maine to keep house for a very exacting brother while his wife went to the hospital. You'll have to get yourself settled, Maggie, one way or another, she had said, or else come with me.

Maggie went to a domestic employment agency the next day, and the moment she set foot in it she was a valuable and interesting client. She was sent out to see Mrs. Mayfield, and Mrs. Mayfield had engaged her there and then. In a way, she thought, it's not such a bad job. I've saved twenty-one dollars out of my first month's pay, and I've learned quite a lot, listening to them talk and all that, and Miss Dolly has been sweet to me. But it's not what I want, and I won't stay.

She put on her black poplin dress and the little ruffled apron and the cap that was a frill with a black velvet band. It was becoming to her; she looked pretty. But she did not *want* to wear a cap and apron. I'm not going to be just a maid, she said to herself. I can do better than this for myself. A *lot* better.

She took out her Manual of Shorthand, and her notebook, and started down the stairs. It was not nearly so bad to meet Mr. Camford in the hall when she was wearing her black uniform and her best shoes; she felt almost professional. Let him come, the mean old thing. . . .

"Maggie!" said a low and lovely voice, and she turned to see Miss Dolly in the doorway of her room. "Come in, will you, Maggie?" she said. "And close the door. I want to speak to you."

A woman of mystery, Miss Dolly was, and Maggie was deeply interested in her. Still young, handsome and elegant, she lived a curious and solitary life here with her aunt and uncle. She never went anywhere except sometimes to do a little shopping; no one came here to visit her.

But it had not always been like this. Maggie came in every morning to do the room, and she had found in it souvenirs of a very different kind of life, little things, bottles, boxes, ash-trays from Paris and London, and in the closet were lovely evening dresses and wraps and slippers, gold and silver. Sometimes Miss Dolly would come in while Maggie was busy there, she would sit down and light a cigarette and talk with a vague and melancholy kindness; she would ask Maggie questions about herself, sometimes she gave her a little present, a cake of perfumed soap, some writing paper, an embroidered handkerchief.

"I think she's had some great misfortune," Maggie said to Mrs. Crabtree.

"I don't know about that," Mrs. Crabtree had said. "What I do know is, that she wasn't living here when I first came a year ago. She had a place of her own somewhere, and I never saw her here, and never so much as heard there was such a person till the day she came, bag and baggage, to stay."

"It seems a strange way for anyone like her to live," Maggie had said. "She's very good-looking, don't you think, Mrs. Crabtree?"

"Yes," Mrs. Crabtree had admitted. "Though I must say I don't care for such a dark complexion. It always looks foreign to me. And she talks French; I've heard her on the telephone."

This made her still more interesting.

"Why ever do you suppose she came here to live in such a lonely kind of way?" Maggie had asked.

"I couldn't say," Mrs. Crabtree had answered.

"Mrs. Mayfield and Mr. Camford seem so sort of distant to her," Maggie had continued. "I don't think they're nice to her."

"That's something I shouldn't care to give any opinion on, Maggie," Mrs. Crabtree had said with a trace of severity. "Not knowing the circumstances."

But Maggie went right on having opinions. She looked over at Miss Dolly stretched out on her chaise-longue, supple and languid in her black chiffon negligee, smoking a cigarette, her dark eyes gazing steadily and sadly out of the window. It's some love affair, thought Maggie, waiting there with her Manual under her arm.

She turned her head toward Maggie.

"Maggie," she said, "I can trust you, can't I?"

"Yes, ma'am," said Maggie.

"Ever since you came here, I've been studying you, Maggie," said Miss Dolly, "and I think you're a very remarkable girl."

The color rose in Maggie's cheeks, her heart beat faster, with pleasure and a sort of relief. For this was what she had been waiting for, this praise, this recognition that she was not really just a maid.

"Thank you, Miss Dolly," she said.

"I'm going to translate a French book into English. It's a wonderful book and I think it'll make a sensation. I'm going away to the country to work on it, and I want you to come with me as my secretary."

This was almost too good to be true.

"Miss Dolly . . . *Thank* you," said Maggie, a little unsteadily. "I haven't had much—I haven't had any real experience, but I can type pretty well. I'm a good speller—"

"I know you're just the right person for me," said Miss Dolly. "You're young—how old are you, Maggie?"

"Nineteen, Miss Dolly."

"That *is* young, isn't it?" said Miss Dolly with a faint

9

smile. "But I think you're very understanding, Maggie. I think we'll have a wonderful summer."

"Yes, Miss Dolly," said Maggie. "When did you think of going, Miss?"

"I've got to go to-night."

"*To-night!*" said Maggie.

"Yes. There's a car coming for me."

"But Miss Dolly, I've got to give Mrs. Mayfield notice."

"She can easily find somebody else, Maggie."

"Yes, I know, Miss Dolly, but—well, I'm sure she wouldn't discharge me without notice, and I don't feel I ought to do that to her."

"We can arrange that."

"Shall I speak to her now, Miss Dolly, and see what she thinks?"

"No," said Miss Dolly, and fell silent for a time. "Maggie," she said, "I don't want my aunt or my uncle or *anyone* to know we're going."

"But, Miss Dolly!" cried Maggie. "You mean for me just to go, just to walk out, and not even tell Mrs. Crabtree?"

"Maggie, I've *got* to go to-night," said Miss Dolly, "and I've got to go—without anyone knowing. You can take my word for it, can't you, that I've got a good reason?"

"Yes, Miss Dolly, but—"

"But what?"

Maggie was almost too miserable to answer. This thing *was* too good to be true. Lots of things were. I ought to've known there'd be a catch to it, somewhere, she thought.

"Maggie," said Miss Dolly, "I'm going to trust you utterly. Hand me my bag, will you? Read this, Maggie." She took a typewritten letter out of an envelope and handed it to Maggie.

"Dolly, you Devil:

I'm not going to wait any longer. To-morrow I'm coming to the house—with a bottle of vitriol. Then you won't sneer at me any more, devil that you are.

Othello."

"But, Miss Dolly!" said Maggie, astounded. "It's some kind of joke, isn't it?"

"No," said Miss Dolly.

"But, Miss Dolly, if anybody means that—"

"He does mean it," said Miss Dolly.

"But then, Miss Dolly, you ought to tell somebody. Mr. Camford—"

"He's the last person I'd ever tell. He and my aunt would turn me out of the house if they knew anything about this, and they'd take all my money."

"They couldn't do that, Miss Dolly. Nobody's allowed—"

"Yes, they could. I've signed all sorts of papers . . . Maggie, you *must* have noticed how it is here for me, how unwelcome I am. In this house—the house I was born in. It was my father's house, Maggie, and he meant me to have it. But I was very young—and very foolish. . . . I was so happy here with my mother and father when I was a child—and maybe that's not a very good preparation for the world. . . . My parents were so gay and generous and loving . . . I didn't realize how different other people were. I trusted people—too much."

There were stars in her dark eyes, and Maggie felt very sorry for her—in a way. But she was more shocked than touched.

"Do you mean they—other people—have got your house and your money away from you, Miss Dolly?" she asked.

"Oh, I wouldn't *care* about that if they were only kind and understanding," said Miss Dolly.

"You have to care about things like that," said Maggie briefly. "You have to look out for yourself—"

"I'm not like that," said Miss Dolly. "I just want to get away, Maggie. I just want a little peace and quiet."

"But, Miss Dolly, that man, the one that wrote the letter, he'll find out where you are, and he'll come after you."

"He won't, if nobody here knows where I've gone. Oh Maggie, please don't argue any more! Please just be kind and friendly and come with me. Things are worse, much worse than you imagine. I'll tell you later, when we're out of this horrible house. Maggie, you're so sensible and well-behaved. I need you so. Won't you come with me, Maggie?"

What a strange thing, that anyone like Miss Dolly, beautiful and rich and aristocratic, should be begging and praying Maggie MacGowan to come away with her! It's like a story, Maggie thought. I know I'm sensible. I know if there's one thing I am, it's practical. I do know how to look out for myself and I dare say I could help Miss Dolly in more ways than one. I suppose she sort of felt that, by instinct.

Miss Dolly had laid the back of her hand against her forehead, her eyes were closed, one hand dropped over the arm of the chair; she looked exhausted and curiously helpless. Look what she's got herself into, thought Maggie. There's this man threatening to throw vitriol at her—and she's signed these papers and lost her house and her money. My goodness!

"Will you come, Maggie?" asked Miss Dolly.

"Yes, miss," said Maggie.

"Oh Maggie, I'm so glad! I'll talk everything over with you once we're away from here. Maggie, the car's coming at half-past eleven. Just pack what you'll need for a day or two, and meet me at the back door. I'm so glad, Maggie . . ."

TWO

I'M DOING the right thing, to go with Miss Dolly, Maggie said to herself. She's in a great deal of trouble, and she needs me.

But just the same, she felt mean.

Mrs. Crabtree had gone up to her room for her afternoon rest, leaving the kitchen as neat as a pin, the dessert was all made and in the ice-box, the lettuce was washed and in a sieve, the leg of lamb stood on the table ready for the oven. Always leave your meat *out* of the ice-box two or three hours before you cook it, she had told Maggie.

It was quiet as the grave down here, not a sound but the loud ticking of the clock. Through the barred window you could see feet going by along the street, cracked old shoes, and gleaming new ones, gay high-heeled pumps and a child's little stubby brown shoes. Sometimes a truck passed with a hollow roar, shaking the walls, the windows rattled in a gust of wind. Mrs. Crabtree's newspaper lay neatly folded in the rocking-chair, and Maggie sat down to read it for a while.

There was a picture of that Mrs. Amber; pretty she was, and young. It's funny there's never a word about Mr. Amber, thought Maggie. Well, maybe she wasn't really married at all. Brought it on herself , . . ? They all do, Mrs. Crabtree said, getting mixed up with men. . . . Miss Dolly must have got mixed up some way with the man who wrote that letter, Othello. Well, that was Desdemona's husband, and he smothered her with a pillow. Vitriol . . . That's a terrible thing. It blinds you and eats away your flesh. . . . I don't think she realizes how serious it is. I don't think she realizes anything much. She's so helpless. She needs someone to look after her.

She sighed, and put down the paper and opened the Shorthand Manuel. It's going to be wonderful experience, working on Miss Dolly's book, she thought. Maybe later on I can get to be a secretary for a famous author. I'll get to tea parties where there are famous people. Who knows? I might even marry a great author.

At half-past five Mrs. Crabtree descended in a clean print dress; she moved about, amiable, superbly adequate.

"Just the three of them for dinner," she observed. "I never like to work for three. Two is all right, and four is all right, and more than four. But three is awkward."

Maggie set the table as Mrs. Mayfield wanted it; real old-fashioned, she would not have any of the nice things you saw in the magazines. A fine damask cloth, the ornate old silver, the French china with a band of deep blue and gold, and right in the middle a white bowl of red carnations. A few moments before seven, Mrs. Mayfield herself came into the dining-room in a black dinner dress, a tall woman with an ungainly stoop forward from the waist, and dark hair grizzled at the temples. She looked at the table in her peering, absent-minded way.

"You're learning to do very nicely, Maggie," she said. "You can light the candles now."

Maggie lit the four candles in the chased silver holders, and the family entered. Mr. Camford, in a dark purple smoking-jacket, sat at the foot and his sister opposite him and poor Miss Dolly at the side. She had a queer look to-night, Maggie thought; maybe because she had her raven-black hair brushed back from her forehead, making her face look thinner, almost worn; or maybe it was because she had come to the table in a yellow sweater and a short skirt.

Mrs. Mayfield began to talk about a book she had just finished reading, she told about it firmly and clearly, and her brother listened with attention. No wonder, thought Maggie. She's got such an interesting way of telling about things, and she knows such a lot. Miss Dolly's very well educated and speaks French and all that, but she can't hold her own with those two. Not about books and things like that.

The rope of the dumb-waiter slapped gently against the wall; that was Mrs. Crabtree's signal that the entrée was coming up. Everything served just right, the leg of lamb carved in juicy slices, the vegetables in covered dishes, the plates warmed, the mint jelly solid.

I guess this is the last time, Maggie thought as she stood at the sideboard, and a curious pang of regret shot through her. It's *nice*, she thought, looking at the table with the candles and the red carnations. She knew every fork and spoon, every plate and glass; for six months she had been handling them with care and even affection. And I *like* to hear Mr. Camford and Mrs. Mayfield talk, she thought. I know they're mean to Miss Dolly, but they've got something.

"Maggie!" said Mr. Camford reproachfully. "*Water*, please!"

He felt strongly about having to ask for water. Mr. Camford liked observant service, Mrs. Mayfield had said. And he's right, Maggie thought, filling his glass and looking down at his bald head with new indulgence. Well, I guess I'll never see him again.

She had her own dinner in the kitchen with Mrs. Crabtree, and it was cosy. Mrs. Crabtree was particular, too; they had a nice clean tablecloth and napkins, their plates were warmed, too. They ate just what the others did, only instead of coffee they had a big brown pot of tea.

"The grocer's boy had a late paper," said Mrs. Crabtree, "said he found it. He left it for me. He's a nice boy. There's more about that Mrs. Amber in it, and you can see it's the way I said. She brought it on herself. Divorced, she was, and living all by herself, except for this colored maid. And she had these cocktail parties that lasted half the night, and so on. A gay life, as they call it."

She washed the dishes, and Maggie dried them.

"Well . . ." said Mrs. Crabtree after she had locked the iron gate to the area and seen to all the windows. "I'll leave the paper for you, Maggie. I'm off to bed."

"Good night, Mrs. Crabtree."

"Good night, Maggie."

I'm not going to read about Mrs. Amber, Maggie thought. I'm sick and tired of it. And I've got other things to think about.

She was supposed to remain on duty until ten o'clock in case the doorbell rang. Well, it was after nine now, and she thought she could well use the interval in planning what she should take. Her bag was small, and there was so little that could be got into it that her planning was soon done.

Then, to fill in the last moments, she picked up Mrs. Crabtree's newspaper. Clubman Sought in Amber Slaying. And a picture of Mrs. Amber, smiling. She had been found dead, shot, lying on the floor or her bedroom, partially clad, the papers said. I'm sick of that case! Maggie cried to herself, and turned to the editorial page. She read the editorials every day, all of them, to improve herself.

Ten o'clock. She gave the neat cosy kitchen a last look, and turned out the light; she went upstairs to the parlor floor. Mr. Camford was in the drawing-room nearby, but the other rooms were empty; she went on up to the top floor and began to pack the little bag of imitation crocodile, very soft. She had decided to wear the black poplin dress she had on, and she packed her cap and little apron, and a clean morning uniform. Miss Dolly had said she was to be a secretary and not a maid, but there might be little things to do.

When the bag was packed, she sat down to read her book, *Anna Karenina*. It was one of the classics she was determined to read; it interested her and exasperated her. She left her door ajar, and at eleven o'clock she heard Mr. Camford mounting the stairs. The house was quiet now, very quiet.

Her heart beat fast, her hands were cold as ice. Oh, suppose I met Mr. Camford or Mrs. Mayfield *now?* she thought. Sneaking downstairs with a bag. . . . Whatever could I say to them? Or suppose Mrs. Crabtree came out now to the bathroom and saw me? I don't think it can be *right*, to do anything that makes you feel so terrible.

So guilty. She put on the round felt hat and the grey coat, and bag in hand started down the stairs. What'll I say if anybody catches me? I ought to have something ready to say. . . . Well I can't. I won't. I'll say—I'm going away, that's all. Nobody can stop me.

Nobody tried to stop her. She went past the closed doors of the bedrooms and down to the lower hall where a dim light burned all night, down into the black basement, stuffy, filled with the warm, stale smells of cooking. She unlocked the door and stood in the little space between the door and the iron gate to the area. It was nice to be out in the air, nice to look out at the quiet upper East Side street with a light on the corner, and cars going by, and now and then someone on foot.

There was a man on the corner with his back to her, a stocky, broad-shouldered man in a brown pull-over and dark trousers; the street light shone on his bare head that was silvery white. She looked at him idly, wondering what he was doing there, then she looked back over her shoulder, she listened for the sound of Miss Dolly's footsteps. A gust of wind blew through the barred gate, damp and chilly, there were no stars in the sky. Not much of a night for a drive, she thought. I hope it's not a long way.

The man was still standing there; what could he be doing? I wish I had a watch, Maggie thought. As soon as I can save up more, I'll get one. Whatever is that man doing? Could he be that *Othello?*

A sound behind her made her her start; she saw the beam of an electric torch across the kitchen floor.

"Maggie!" said Miss Dolly's voice.

"I'm here, Miss Dolly."

Miss Dolly came to her side and set down her bag.

"It weighs a ton," she said. "Oh, there's Neely! Open the gate, will you, Maggie?"

Maggie opened the gate, and Miss Dolly went out leaving her bag behind her. Ah, well . . . said Maggie, and picked up both the bags and followed her.

Miss Dolly and the silver-haired man had moved aside from the circle of light; they were going round the corner talking to each other, a queer couple, Maggie thought. The man was so kind of poor-looking, and Miss Dolly so stylish in her short fur jacket and her narrow black skirt, her black turban, her high-heeled shoes. The chauffeur, he must be.

There was a car drawn up to the curb, a big, old-fashioned car; the man got in behind the wheel, and Miss Dolly stood waiting for Maggie.

"Will you sit in the back, Maggie?" she said. "I want to talk to Neely."

There was a glass partition behind the front seat; Maggie, alone in the back, was shut off in silence and a moldy darkness. I's a funny feeling, not to know where you're going she thought.

She looked at Miss Dolly and she was astonished. The light on the dashboard showed her face all alive and sparkling; she was smiling, talking to that driver, and he was talking to her. Not like a lady and a chauffeur. Well, maybe he wasn't a chauffeur, but the owner of the car, only he looked so sort of poor.

It came into her head then, that, after all, she knew very

little about Miss Dolly, and nothing at all about her friends. A very funny feeling it was not to know where you were going, or who you were going with.

THREE

THEY WERE out of the city, driving along a wide boulevard, when the rain began dashing against the window, drumming on the top of the car. The two straight rows of lights ahead twinkled through a veil of falling water, the flat countryside was blotted out, the cars and trucks that passed them went with a blurred rush.

Maggie leaned back in a corner, chilled and depressed. She was in the habit of going to bed early, and she closed her eyes and fell asleep now. But only for a little time; she waked with a start, and there was the rain and the black flat countryside, and Miss's vivid happy face turned again to the driver.

She dozed again, and waked when the car began to jolt over a road full of ruts. There were trees here and no lights, the car slipped and struggled in mud. It's just miserable not to know where you're going or where you are, she thought. If I even knew what time it was . . . I wish I had a watch.

That bothered her more than anything, that feeling of blank and unlimited time. Suppose I've been asleep for hours? she thought. Suppose it's to-morrow night? Well, it isn't. I mustn't be silly. There's Miss Dolly right in front of me. She's somebody I *know*. There's nothing queer about her. She just wants to get away from that man, and get a little peace and quiet in the country. That's natural.

She's pretty friendly with that driver. . . . Maybe he's a friend of hers. He's got white hair, but he doesn't look old. He's got a hole in the elbow of his sweater. Well, that's nothing. Some people don't care. I've heard about millionaires that look like regular tramps.

She made an effort to go to sleep, she leaned back and closed her eyes. But the road was very bad now, she was jounced and shaken, she felt the car skid and slew around,

17

she opened her eyes and the car stopped. The white-haired man was getting out.

There was nothing here, nothing but rain and the dark. She thought something must have gone wrong with the car, nothing serious because Miss Dolly sat smoking there, with no gesture of alarm or even curiosity. The rain dashed against the windows as if flung from a bucket; it was surprising to think of the white-haired man out in it without hat or coat.

And then a light sprang up and outlined a window, she could see the dark bulk of a house. In a moment the man came back, running, with a blanket held against his breast; he opened the door to the front seat, and Maggie saw Miss Dolly laugh, her teeth white against her rouged lips. She moved over, and the man put the blanket over her head and around her shoulders, he took her arm and helped her out.

Maggie sat close to the window; she saw them run along a path and up the steps of a little porch, the man opened the door and they went in.

Well, have they stopped in to visit somebody? Maggie thought. If I'm a secretary, it's a sort of funny way to treat me, going off and not saying a word. But I never really believed much in all that. She sat there waiting in drowsy discomfort, yawning in the close dampness. Then the door of the house opened and the man appeared in the light, waving his arm as if scooping something out of the air toward his face. She watched him for some time before it occurred to her that he was beckoning to her.

Well, that's not very polite, she thought, and taking up her little bag she opened the door and got out in the pelting rain. It was too dark and too slippery to run, she went cautiously along the path and up the steps.

"Look here!" said the man. "Get something for Miss Camford to eat, will you? Just a little snack—coffee—anything. Here's the kitchen. Take anything you see."

His hair was not white, but a pale blond; he was young, with a broad, strong-boned face, and pale eyes that rested on her for a moment with impersonal coolness.

"Here's the kitchen," he said again. "Call me if you want anything."

She went into the room he pointed at, a dim and dirty kitchen lit by a feeble bulb hanging from the ceiling, with a bare wooden floor, an oil-stove furry with grease, a narrow iron sink. She set down her bag and looked around her, and narrowed her eyes to keep from crying.

All right! she said to herself. All right! I was a fool to come. I might have known . . . But here she was, and she accepted the consequences grimly. She opened her little bag and put on her apron, she looked around and found a paper bag of coffee, she found a battered old aluminum coffee pot; there was a small wooden ice-box in a corner, and in it she found ham, and butter and eggs, and some ants running around. I wouldn't work for the woman who runs *this* house, thought Maggie, not for fifty dollars a week. I never saw—

"For God's sake . . ." said a voice behind her, and she turned quickly. A man in a dressing-gown stood in the doorway, a big, sun-burned, grey-eyed man, staring at her, and yawning like a big cat. "For God's sake, who are you?" he asked.

"I'm—I came with Miss Camford," said Maggie briefly.

"Susanne," he said. "The dainty little French maid."

"I'm not French," said Maggie.

The man ran his fingers through his dark hair, and it stood out like feathers behind his ears; he leaned against the doorway, and Maggie noticed with disfavor that his feet were bare.

"You're pretty," he said earnestly. "You're the cutest little trick I *ever* saw. Red hair, too. Are you saucy?"

With all her heart she resented his words, his tone, the way he was staring at her. She went on with her work, trying to ignore him.

"I bet you slap people," he said. "Fresh guys. Piff. Paff. Pouff. Non?"

There was a loaf of bread on a shelf, not wrapped, just out there in the dust. It was stale, too, hard as a rock, she sawed away at it with a knife.

"You're pretty," he said, "but not very polite. After all, when a pretty little girl all dressed up like Susanne suddenly appears in my kitchen in the middle of the night, I think she ought to speak."

"Is it your kitchen?" said Maggie.

"Half of it's mine," he said. "It happens to be the half you're in now."

"Where do you want supper served, please?" asked Maggie.

"What supper?" he said. "The only thing is, you ought to wear silk stockings instead of cotton. . . ."

She looked at him with scorn in her blue eyes.

"Aha!" he said. "I knew you were saucy."

This was too much for her.

"I'm not saucy," she said. "I'm here doing the work I'm paid to do—and minding my own business. If you feel like standing there and making fun of me, I can't stop you."

He straightened up.

"I wasn't making fun of you," he said. "That's just a cheap idiot way I have. Meant to be amusing . . . Meant to hide my sensitive spirit. Cassidy is the name. Johnny Cassidy."

The kettle was boiling and she made the coffee; she began to butter the rock-like bread, and to make ham sandwiches. She was not a bit tired or confused now; she was deft and quick and perfectly sure of herself and she felt ready to go on working for hours in a sort of rage. I'd like to scrub the floor, she thought, and clean up this nasty dirty place. That man can stand there staring just as long as he likes. I don't care.

"Oh, Maggie!" said Miss Dolly's voice. "Oh, you *poor* child! What *are* you doing?"

"Getting some supper, Miss Dolly."

"But it's three o'clock, Maggie. You must be worn out."

"I'm not tired, Miss Dolly."

"You're not to do another thing," said Miss Dolly. "Come on, and I'll show you your room."

"I'll just finish—"

"You come along this minute," said Miss Dolly, and took her hand.

"May I ask for an introduction?" murmured Johnny Cassidy.

"This is my secretary, Miss MacGowan," said Miss Dolly, with more than a trace of curtness. "Do come along now, Maggie. What put it into your head to start all this at such an hour?"

"The—other gentleman asked me to," said Maggie.

"Neely?" said Miss Dolly. "Oh, he hasn't any sense of time at all. This way, Maggie."

Maggie picked up her bag from the corner, and Johnny Cassidy took it from her.

"No, thank you," she said. "I'd rather—"

But he went ahead of her out of the kitchen and up a steep and narrow stair; he mounted these, limber and nimble in his bare feet. He put the bag in a room and came out, and stood aside.

20

"Good night, Miss MacGowan," he said.

Miss Dolly closed the door and they both looked around them at the room. It was a big room, low-ceilinged, furnished with a big divan, a wicker chair, a bamboo table, some shelves of books, and a tall old-fashioned radio cabinet. Here too, the only light was from a bulb hung from the rafters; it was gloomy, shadowy, smelling of mold.

"We can fix it up to-morrow," said Miss Dolly. She crossed the room to the divan and pressed it with her hand. "It *seems* very comfortable," she said. "My room is just in here through this door, and the bathroom is just across the hall."

"Thank you, miss," said Maggie.

"Don't call me 'miss' any more. Call me Dolly, won't you, Maggie?"

"I'll try to," said Maggie.

"It's going to be nice here, don't you think, Maggie?"

"Well, it's hard to judge yet, Miss Dolly."

"Please call me Dolly! We're going to have a wonderful summer here, Maggie. We'll change things, and make the place charming."

"Excuse me, Miss Dolly, but—isn't there any—any lady of the house?"

"No," said Miss Dolly. "It's Neely's house. He's an artist, you know, and very talented. I didn't know Johnny Cassidy would be here. But I don't think he'll stay long. He never stays anywhere."

"There's just Mr. Cassidy and Mr. Neely?"

"Curtius. Cornelius Curtius. He's a Dutchman, Maggie, from Holland. You'll like him."

"Yes, miss."

"But you will call me Dolly, won't you? You've come here as my friend, Maggie."

"I'll try," said Maggie.

"Let's go to bed," said Miss Dolly. "We're both tired."

She smiled at Maggie a little anxiously, and after a moment she went off into the room that opened out of this big one. She came back almost at once.

"Maggie, could you possibly help me with the bed? It seems so queer."

There was nothing at all in the little room but a white iron double bed and a chest of drawers. And the bed was queer because the covers were not tucked in, but just folded on top of it. Maggie made it neatly while Dolly began to undress.

"Now I'll go and wash," said Miss Dolly, "and then I won't have to disturb you by going through your room again."

She had left her things scattered all over, her lovely delicate underwear, her little gold watch and her sapphire bracelet tangled up in her stockings on the chest of drawers. Maggie made the room as neat as she could before Miss Dolly came back. She looked surprisingly pretty and glowing, in a white terry robe, her black hair loose about her olive-skinned face.

"It's going to be lovely here, Maggie!" she said.

"Yes, miss," said Maggie. "Good night!"

She went back to the big room, closing the door softly behind her. She was not going to take off even her apron when she went to the bathroom to wash, not she! Not when she and Miss Dolly were alone in this house with those two men. Queer men . . .

She returned to the big room, and she wanted to lock the door. There was no key in the lock, no bolt. She fixed a chair under the knob, and took the faded green cover off the divan. Nothing under it but a mattress, no sheets, no blankets, nothing at all.

She did cry a little then, but while the tears ran down her freshly-scrubbed cheeks, she was busy. She put the green cover back, she fluffed up the pillows, she took off her apron, her black dress, her shoes, she put on her dark-blue dressing-gown and her felt slippers, she brushed her hair, one hundred strokes, and then she went to the shelves to get a book. For she had decided to sit up all night.

She found a novel that seemed nice, and she found a tabloid newspaper of yesterday's date. She sat down in a chair, determined to read, and the first thing she saw in the paper was a picture of the murdered Mrs. Amber, smiling, with her hair in a cloud about her face. Police of Two Cities Seek Clubman for Questioning, she read; and there was a picture of the Clubman, looking as he ought to look, dark and handsome, with a neat little moustache. Arthur Curran, Socialite and Sportsman, Evaded Police in New York and Boston To-day. Friends think he has gone to Florida to avoid publicity in connection with the death of Mrs. Sally Amber, found partially clad.

I'm sick and tired of that case, Maggie thought. She brought it on herself, Mrs. Crabtree said. . . . They all do, she said. . . . By getting mixed up with some man, one way or another.

And what's Miss Dolly doing?

Coming out here to this nasty dirty queer house with these two men in it. What kind of men *are* they, I'd like to know? They could be blackmailers—or anything. I don't believe Miss Dolly's any judge. She seems so happy . . . I never saw her smiling and laughing before . . . I suppose she thinks she's safe now.

Well, I don't. No key in the door. I hope to goodness there isn't any kind of balcony outside the window, she thought, and rose hastily. There were some french windows at one end of the room; they would be the dangerous ones. There was a key in the lock there, she tried it and pulled the window open. And there was a balcony; the light gleamed on wet planks.

She put on her shoes and threw her coat over her shoulders, because she wanted to see, she would see, what there was out there. The rain drove at her in a slanting sheet and she stepped carefully to the railing. She saw no lights, no trees, only the dark sky. She glanced down, and there, directly beneath her she saw a sheet of black water. She could hear it lapping against the wall underneath the planks where she stood.

A house—right *in* the water . . .? She leaned over the rail, staring, half-incredulous, but it was true; that was water, moving water. Something flounced in it, making a little curl of white; something alive.

She went back into the room and locked the window, and because everything was so dreadful and so miserable, she rebelled against it. Nothing to be afraid of, she told herself, sharply. She knelt down and said her prayers, and turned out the light.

The big room was black as the pit. Very well. Everybody goes to sleep in the dark except cowards. Still in her dressing-gown and slippers, she lay down on the divan. The wind came in gusts, the rain spattered against the windows, and when a little lull came, she could hear the water lapping against the wall.

All right. She wasn't afraid of water. If something flounced again, it was a fish. Natural for there to be fish in the water, and I suppose night is the same as day to them, she thought. It'll be morning pretty soon. I'll get some sleep, and the first thing it'll be light again.

She felt cold, and she curled herself up in her coat. The wind blew and the rain poured down, and the dark water lapped, and she went to sleep.

FOUR

IT'S A miserable thing not to have a watch, thought Maggie. It was certainly day, but the rain still fell, a steady drizzle now from the grey sky; it might be early morning, and it might be late. Back in New York you could tell by the sounds from the street; here there were no sounds, not even the lapping of the water any more.

She put on her clean blue cotton dress to go to the bathroom; she took it off to wash and put it on again. She was not going to meet those men in any dressing-gown. Then when she was all neat and trim, she went down the narrow stairs, quietly but not timidly. She felt that she had been deceived and shabbily treated; 'put upon,' she called it in her mother's phrase, and that warmed her heart with a good, steady anger.

The nasty dirty house was chillier and mustier than ever; she went through the room at the foot of the stairs, glancing at it with scorn, a sort of dining-room it was with a cheap golden oak sideboard cluttered with unbelievable things; she saw a red satin slipper there, two empty brandy bottles, a dying purple flower in a pot, a blue lustre horse, an iron bank modeled after the Statue of Liberty. Plenty of other things too, but she did not trouble to examine them, she went on into the kitchen, and it was just as she had left it last night; no one had touched the coffee or the sandwiches, nothing had been put away.

She put on the kettle to make tea, and then she opened the back door. There was a little porch out there and a sort of wooden tunnel roofed over by the upper story of the house and filled with dark, lapping water. On one side a ramp led up to a steep bank, there was an iron stanchion there to which a rowboat was tied, and beside this was a little launch at anchor.

And through the tunnel she could see a path of water running through flat marshes; everything was flat and grey and empty. But the damp air was salty and good, she was glad to breathe it, she was glad to see a gull swoop low over the reeds. This was a place you could get out of, it was lonely enough, strange enough, but it was no longer a nightmare.

She left the door open while she ate her breakfast of tea and stale bread. It did not seem to her proper to take any of the other food in the kitchen; only bread was always proper, it was what you had a right to take. Now then . . . she thought. I don't know . . . I'll wash the things I've used myself, of course; but I don't know if I'll clean up this nasty kitchen before I go, or not.

Go she would, as soon as Miss Dolly waked up, no matter how much she talked about being a secretary, and having a lovely summer. Of course I can't ever go back to Mrs. Mayfield now, after going away like that without a word, she thought, and maybe she won't even give me a reference. But I guess I can get another position like that in a *nice* house, and I've got twenty dollars saved up. I guess I could make out for two weeks if I have to.

The prospect did not daunt her in the least; she would have gone back to New York with a half, with a quarter as much money, and not been seriously worried. She *knew* she was a good worker, she knew she could do things people were glad to pay for; she was young, healthy, nimble, and she had great faith in herself. I'll walk to a railroad station if I have to, she thought; but this very day, back I go.

She looked at the sink, narrowing her eyes. Oh, well . . . she thought. I will clean up everything. I've just got to, that's all. She filled the kettle again, and she had begun to rinse the dishes when there was a knock at the door. As a matter of course she dried her hands and went to open it.

A taxi was just driving away, and a man stood on the porch, a portly, clean-shaven, white-haired man with a square jaw and stern blue eyes.

"Will you kindly tell Miss Camford that Mr. Angel is here," he said.

"Miss Camford isn't up yet, sir," said Maggie.

"I'm sorry," he said, "but I'm afraid I shall have to disturb her. If you'll tell her that Mr. Angel is here—"

"Does she—excuse me, sir; but will she know the name?"

He smiled a little.

"Undoubtedly," he said. "I am Miss Camford's lawyer."

A fine looking man, and handsomely dressed, a man to be credited. "Will you step in, sir?" said Maggie. "This room isn't very tidy, sir, but we just got here."

Mr. Angel looked about him at the dining-room with a distaste that pleased Maggie, he took off his hat, and he was drawing off his grey gloves as she started up the stairs.

Miss Camford's lawyer? she thought. Well, somebody's found out where she is, and pretty quick, too. Well, it's a good thing. I hope they make her leave here. It's no place for her. She knocked on the door of Miss Dolly's room, and getting no answer, she opened the door. And she was somehow touched by the look of Miss Dolly asleep with her black hair spread out on the pillow, and her face so pretty and so serene.

"Miss Dolly! I'm sorry, but Mr. Angel's here, Miss Dolly!"

Miss Dolly opened her eyes and looked blankly up at Maggie.

"What?" she said.

"Mr. Angel is here, Miss Dolly."

"Mr. Angel?" she repeated. "But, Maggie!" She sat up in her lovely ivory silk nightgown with a yoke of écru lace. "Mr. Angel? But he *couldn't* be!"

"Well, he is, Miss Dolly," said Maggie.

"But—where is he, Maggie?"

"He's in that dining-room, Miss Dolly."

"Maggie, are the boys with him?"

"The boys, miss?"

"Neely and Johnny. Are they talking to him?"

"No, miss. I don't think they're up yet. They didn't get any breakfast for themselves anyhow."

"Let me think a moment . . ." said Miss Dolly. "Wait . . . Maggie. Bring Mr. Angel upstairs."

"Up *here*?" said Maggie in stern astonishment.

"Yes. Up to the sitting-room. The room you slept in. Hurry up, Maggie! And don't tell the others he's here until I've had a chance to talk to him. Hurry up, Maggie!"

And why? thought Maggie. What's all this hurry and worry about, I'd like to know?

"Maggie, hurry!"

"Yes, ma'am," said Maggie without any expression.

She closed the door as she went out, and she took time to tidy that room, to put everything belonging to her out of sight; then she went down to Mr. Angel. She found him standing with his hands behind him looking at the sideboard.

"I suppose you have a telephone here," he said.

"I don't know, sir," said Maggie.

"I hope so," he said. "I shall want it to send for a taxi presently. I'm obliged to be back in New York for an appointment. That's why I came at such an early hour. Miss Camford coming down soon?"

"She'd like you to come upstairs, please, sir."

"Upstairs?" he repeated, with a look that Maggie observed with understanding and sympathy. "Miss Camford—er—she's not feeling well?"

"There's a kind of sitting-room upstairs, sir," said Maggie. "This way, please."

She led him into that sitting-room, and knocked at the bedroom door.

"Maggie?" said Miss Dolly. "Come in!"

She was wearing a dark-red housecoat with a high collar, and her hair was tied back from her forehead with a ribbon to match; she looked wonderfully tired and gentle, and wonderfully young.

"Look, Maggie!" she said. "Here's a little note for Neely. His room is the first door on the right beside the stairs. I'm asking him to drive you down to the drug store right away to get this prescription filled."

"Miss Dolly . . . If he could go by himself . . . I haven't got the dishes washed yet."

"That doesn't matter. I'd rather you took the prescription for me, Maggie."

Well, if it's something sort of confidential . . . thought Maggie. But how much she did not want to go knocking at that Neely's door! How much she hated all of this, the dirt, the disorder, the general queerness . . . She knocked, and he called out at once. "Who is it?"

"It's—me," she answered.

He opened the door, and she was relieved to see that he was dressed. "Oh, it's you!" he said. "Miss—what is it?"

"MacGowan," said Maggie. "Here's a note for you from Miss Camford, Mr. Curtius."

He unfolded the piece of paper and read it.

"All right!" he said. "Come along."

"I'll get my hat and coat, Mr. Curtius."

"Don't bother," he said impatiently.

"I won't be a minute," said she.

"Dolly wants the medicine at once," he said. "I'll wait for you outside in the car."

She knocked at the sitting-room door and there was no answer. She knocked again and waited, knocked louder. Well, for goodness sake, she thought. Has she gone and got him into the bedroom? She opened the door and entered and the room was empty. All right! she thought. It's none of my business. She got her hat and coat out of the closet, and then as she turned away, she saw Mr. Agel out on the balcony, standing by the rail. The rain had stopped, the grey sky was growing light. He had his hands clasped behind his back again, his white head was raised; he looked sort of noble, she thought, like a senator, or something.

She ran down the stairs and out of the house, and Neely was sitting at the wheel of the big car. For a moment, Maggie hesitated, but he did not open the door or suggest her sitting in front with him, so she got into the back seat. She could see now how isolated that queer house was, standing almost in that river that was not exactly a river but a slow current winding through the marshes.

They turned away from that and along a road slippery with mud, and lined with fields of grass yellow and stunted; no trees, no houses. But when the sun came out, this flat and empty world grew gay, there were dandelions and clover, there was a sweet freshness in the air. They came presently to a highway and filling stations, and diners and a little house here and there, and then they came to a street in a village, tree-shaded, tranquil, with a public library behind a grass lawn, a squat, white-pillared post office, a drug store on the corner. Neely stopped the car, and Maggie got out. I like it here, she thought. This is a nice place.

A thin man in his shirt-sleeves, with spectacles a little down from the bridge of his nose, took the prescription and studied it.

"Take me half an hour," he said. "D'you want to wait?"

"Yes, thank you," said Maggie. "Could I get a soda?"

"Yes," he said calmly.

Neely sat down beside her with his hands in his pockets. "What's wrong with Dolly?" he asked.

"I don't know," said Maggie.

She did not care for Neely, she did not like the careless way he dressed, she did not like his rude, indifferent ways; she glanced at him and found his pale-blue eyes looking her up and down with no light in them.

"You have good bones," he said.

Well, if that's all he finds to admire in me . . . thought Maggie. Bones . . . The druggist had set the chocolate soda before her, and she began to drink it through a straw, giving it her whole attention.

"I'll come back for you," said Neely abruptly, and went out of the store; through the window she saw him get into the car and drive away.

Well, I don't know . . . Maggie thought, sipping the soda. It's certainly not what I expected. I just hate that house, and I don't like these two men, but still . . . It's experience, and if I help Miss Dolly with her book it'll be a reference, and I can get a really nice job. It's queer, and Miss Dolly's acting queer, I must say, getting so lively and cheerful all of a sudden. You'd think she'd forgotten all about that letter about the vitriol. . . . If Mr. Angel could find out so quickly where she had gone, that Othello man might find out too. . . . I don't know. There are lots of things I don't like, but I'll guess I'll stay.

"Here's your eye lotion, miss," said the druggist. "Forty-five cents, that'll be."

Maggie took the bottle and counted out the money. Eye lotion? she thought. Sending me off in such a hurry for *that?* I never heard her say anything about any trouble with her eyes. No . . . It was just to get that Neely out of the house while Mr. Angel was there. And I suppose she wanted me to go with him to make it look more reasonable. Well, I don't wonder she didn't want Mr. Angel to see Neely. I don't know what Mrs. Mayfield and Mr. Camford would say if they knew she was living in this nasty dirty house with two men.

She finished the soda very leisurely, and she looked around for a clock, and saw none. "Excuse me," she said to the druggist, "but can you please tell me the time?"

He took a big watch out of his pocket. "It is now—" he said deliberately, "a—ten forty-five." "Thank you!" said Maggie.

She was getting a little tired of looking out of the window; she got up and walked about the store looking at the soap and powders, she took up a booklet about kidney pills, and read the testimonial letters in it, she went back to the window and looked out at the street where two girls in summer dresses went by, arm-in-arm. Neely's taking a long time, it seems to me.

The time grew longer and longer, the sun grew hotter. She did not like to ask the druggist to look at his watch again; she sat on a stool, she got up and went to look at a case full of cigars, the box lids up, displaying colored pictures of Indians and beautiful girls in white robes with long black hair, reclining under palm trees. A whistle began to blow.

"Excuse me," she said to the druggist, "but is that for noon?"

"That is the noon whistle over to the mills," he said.

It's certainly time Neely came back, she thought. And what if he doesn't come at all? Why, I don't even know where the house is. I don't know where I'm living. She went out into the street then, and looked up and down; there was a stationer's nearby and she went there and bought a little magazine full of condensed articles. You get a lot of information from things like that, she thought, and if I'm going to be a secretary, I want to be able to talk about what's going on.

She went back to the druggist's and sat down again. The druggist went away, and a dark and gloomy boy in spectacles came to take his place. I'll read this one article about high-lighting your personality, thought Maggie, and then I'll find out how to get back by myself.

But Neely came just before she had finished.

"You were certainly gone a long time," said Maggie.

"What of it?" said Neely. "There's no hurry."

"Speak for yourself," said Maggie. "I've got things to do."

"To wash dishes?"

"No," she said briefly, and they went out and got into the car.

"I don't know why she brought you here," said Neely.

It's none of your business, thought Maggie, and did not answer at all.

They drove the rest of the way in silence; when they reached the house he jumped out and ran up the steps and opened the door. Maggie followed with a proud lack of haste; she looked into the dining-room and the kitchen; nobody was there, she went up the stairs and found no one there either. She started to make Miss Dolly's bed when Neely called from below.

"Maggie, look here! Come here, will you?"

She went into the hall and leaned over the stair railing.

"What do you want?" she said, coldly.

"Can you row a boat?" asked Neely from the doorway.

"Yes," she answered.

"Then, will you row me somewhere?"

"I can't," she said, "I've got work to do."

"It won't take long," he said. "I've got to take a bundle somewhere."

"Take it in the car," she said.

"I'm out of gas," he said. "Come on, please. It's only a little way."

"My goodness!" said Maggie, unsteadily. "You people don't care—*what* you ask me to do."

"I don't know how to row," he said, as if that explained everything.

She had reached a stage in which she would have refused him flatly if it had not been for one thing. She had a passion for small boats. Her father had taught her to row and to paddle when she was a little girl; he had taught her a little about sailing, too, and she had taken to it with ecstasy. But he had died at sea, and there had been no more time or money for recreation.

"All right," she said, "if it's not far."

It was warm now in the afternoon sun and she did not bother with hat or coat. She went out with Neely to the ramp at the foot of which the rowboat lay.

"What's that?" she asked frowning.

"It's a mannikin," he said, "a dummy someone lent me to draw from, and I've got to take it back."

It looked like a body, she thought, that long thing stretched out on the bottom of the boat covered with a tarpaulin. It was queer, but everything these people did was queer. She went down the ramp and got into the boat, sure-footed and happy to feel the lift of it under her feet; she sat down and took the oars, and Neely got in awkwardly. She could look right into the kitchen window.

"I never saw a house so close to the water's edge before," she said.

"It used to be a boat-house," Neely said. "They fixed it up for the summer people."

"Which way do we go?"

"Left," he said, and she began to pull on the oars, easily and strongly, going through the dark tunnel out toward the bright glittering water. The last time I went out with Father . . . she thought. We were so happy that day. . . . If I'd been a boy I'd have gone to sea. I'd have been a captain some day like Father.

They came out of the wooden tunnel, and turning left

they came into a part of the river she had not seen from the house; it was far more like a real river here, with higher banks.

"The current is strong here," she said.

"It's tidal," said Neely. "The tide's running out now."

"Salt water?" she asked.

"Oh, yes," he said.

The sun was hot on her head and shoulders, the breeze was fresh against her face. Oh, this is lovely, she thought. Oh, if only I could make a living doing something like this! I'd never feel tired.

The banks were growing steeper, and now she saw a willow.

"Isn't that pretty!" she cried.

Neely did not answer; he was trying to light a cigarette, but the match blew out, and he threw it into the water. It was quiet here; the sky was so blue. The river made a turn, and the boathouse was lost to sight, there were more trees stirring in the wind. It's lovely! It's lovely! she kept saying to herself.

Neely was trying again to light a cigarette; he stood up straddling the bundle, he swayed clumsily.

"Sit down!" she said, sharply. "You'll tip the boat over."

He lost his footing and fell, grasping the side of the boat and capsizing it. Maggie was tumbled out on the surface of the water, the chill of it made her gasp. She swam a stroke or two, and put her hand on the drifting boat and looked for Neely. He was standing in water up to his waist, just standing.

"Catch those oars!" she shouted, but he did not stir. "Mr. Curtius!" she cried. "Help me to turn the boat over or we'll lose it."

But he didn't do anything. She stood up then, and she shuddered a little to find thick soft mud under her feet. She struggled with the boat, but it was very heavy.

"Why don't you *help* me?" she cried.

With an effort she lifted the boat, but it came down into the water again. Then something drifted by her. It was Mr. Angel, floating on his back, going slowly down the stream; the current caught him, and his arms went back behind his white head as if he stretched and relaxed in great comfort, sinking a little below the surface.

FIVE

"Oh . . . stop him!" she cried.

Neely reached for one of the oars that was floating away; he waded a few steps to catch the other oar. But he didn't even look after Mr. Angel.

"Help me—to get him!" cried Maggie.

"No. He's dead," said Neely.

"He's going out to sea!" she said in horror, and turned to go after him. The mud was too thick; she lost one of her shoes, and the feel of the mud was sickening. She began to swim after Mr. Angel, and in spite of her clothes she went fast, helped by the tide. She came up with him and took hold of his sleeve. A matter of two or three strokes would bring her to the bank and she could get him out of the water.

But a rough hand had seized her by the shoulder and pulled her backward, so that Mr. Angel escaped and went on his way.

"Don't be a fool," said Neely, standing beside her waist-deep in the water. "He's dead."

"I know that," said Maggie. "But I want—"

"You can't do him any good," said Neely, "and you'll do Dolly—and all of us—a lot of harm. Yourself, too."

She was on her feet now in that thick hateful mud; she tried to free herself, but he held her fast.

"I don't *let* him go out to sea!" she said.

"Look here! He had a fit or a stroke or something like that. I found him in the boat dead, so I wanted to get rid of him."

"You ought to know better!" said Maggie. "Let me go! You'll get in a lot more trouble with the police, acting like this. Let me *go!* It's everybody's duty to tell the police—"

"Why?" he asked.

The boat was coming along, and he stopped it. "Let's go home and forget it," he said. "Nothing we can do."

"You're awful!" she said. "I won't do it. I'm going to get Mr. Angel—"

"Angel?" said Neely. "Is that his name? Really his name?

Angel?" He grinned from ear to ear. "Angel's on his way to heaven," he said. "That's a good one."

"You ought to be ashamed of yourself! You let me go this minute. I'm going to get poor Mr. Angel out of the water, and then I'm going to tell the police."

"What makes you such a fool?" said Neely. "Let Dolly have her party, anyhow."

"Party! Her *party!*"

"It's important. She's got important people coming."

Maggie began to struggle in earnest to get away, but he was very strong.

"Stop!" he said, not much interested. "Let's turn the boat over and get into it. Silly to be standing here in the water. You look funny."

"You're not—human," said Mggie.

Mr. Angel was out of sight now; either he had disappeared around the bend of the river, or he had sunk to the bottom.

"Come on. Let's go home," said Neely.

"I'm going to find Mr. Angel," she said, "and you can't stop me."

"I will stop you," said Neely. "I don't want you to find him. I want to go home. I want you to row me back."

"I won't," said Maggie.

"Oh, you're a nuisance!" he said angrily.

He let the oars, which he had held under his arm, drop into the water, he gave the boat a shove, he let Maggie go, and he began to walk toward the bank. "If you tell the police," he called back, "you'll get yourself in a hell of a lot of trouble, and *I'll* say it's all a lie. I'm not going to get mixed up in this for any dead angels."

She stood there in the mud and the cold running water with the sun blazing down upon her, not a house, not a living thing in sight, except the broad-shouldered, sturdy figure of Neely making his way across the marsh. Her teeth were chattering with cold, she clenched them and began to swim after the boat. She reached it and went along beside it sometimes swimming and sometimes wading; she caught the oars and pulled them along with her.

She went round the bend of the river, and the boathouse was in sight. But not Mr. Angel. She could see a long way ahead of her, but not a sign of him. She was utterly alone in the empty, sunny world; she was so cold . . . An idea began to come into her head. She tried to banish it, but in vain. If

34

poor Mr. Angel had sunk to the bottom of the muddy water . . .

She swam the rest of the way, juggling both the boat and the oars, shoving them ahead of her into the dark tunnel underneath the balcony. Even in here she could not, and would not set foot on the bottom. She took the painter of the boat in her teeth and scrambled up the ramp; she made the boat fast and took in the oars. And she did all this because it was not in her to waste or destroy anything, and because she had a particular respect for boats.

Shivering and dripping, limping with one shoe on, she went round to the back door. She took off her shoe then, and wrung out her skirts and went up the stairs to the big room. There was no hot water in the bathroom, and she could not face a cold bath; she scrubbed herself with soap and a damp towel, she put on clean underwear and her felt slippers and the black poplin dress. Now I'll call up the police, she told herself.

She looked upstairs and down for a telephone until there was only one place to look. She knocked at Neely's door.

"Come in!" he said, and she opened the door.

Barefoot and in singlet and dark trousers, he was standing at a high tilted board, drawing with a piece of charcoal.

"Well, did you find your angel?" he asked.

"I'm looking for a telephone," said Maggie, briefly.

He put down the charcoal, and thrust his hands into his pockets, frowning; she noticed that his thick lashes were silvery when the sun touched them.

"My God!" he said. "I think I have a hole in my pocket. I must have dropped that telephone in the water, maybe; isn't that too bad?"

"Do you think there's anything to be funny about?" asked Maggie.

"To cry about then?" he asked. "Too many people getting killed in the world now. If some old fellow has a fit and tumbles down dead in a rowboat, all right. He's lucky. He lived a good long time, and he died easy."

There was something foreign in his speech now, not an accent, but an inflection, a choice of words, he looked foreign, too.

He took up the charcoal and began to draw again, and Maggie left him. She was completely at a loss now. There was undoubtedly a telephone to be found somewhere along the highway; but that was a long long way to go in felt

35

bedroom slippers. It would take a long time, too, and what would be happening to Mr. Angel in the meantime? She felt the sharpest distress to think of him, in all his dignity and decency, hurried off upon that shocking journey. He must be brought back, treated with respect and kindness.

Miss Dolly and that Mr. Cassidy will be back soon, she thought. I'll just have to wait for them, and then they can telephone. In the meantime she could get a little work done. She descended to that kitchen again, angry at it, yet with a certain grim enjoyment in the challenge it offered.

The doorbell rang—she dried her hands and took off her work apron, and went to answer it.

A very stout lady stood on the porch.

"Tell Miss Camford Miss Plummer is here," she said affably.

"I'm sorry, ma'am, but Miss Camford isn't in just now," said Maggie.

"She ought to be back by this time," said the other. "Well, I'll come in and wait."

She was a cheerful and amiable lady, dark-haired, in a gay print dress and a dark coat, and sensible low-heeled shoes, and a straw hat coming far down on her face. She looked funny, so stout and in such bright colors, but she looked, Maggie thought, like a lady.

"Miss Camford didn't leave any word for me?" she asked.

"No, ma'am," said Maggie, and Miss Plummer entered the house.

"Mon dieu!" she cried stopping in the doorway of the dining-room.

She turned to Maggie. "Do you know—?" she asked, "What they've done with all my things?"

"No, ma'am," Maggie answered. "I just came yesterday."

"What's your name, my dear?"

"It's Maggie, ma'am."

"Irish!" cried Miss Plummer.

"No, ma'am," said Maggie. "I'm Scotch. On both sides."

"Oh, dear . . ." and Miss Plummer. "Edinburgh . . . A magic city . . . What can they have done with the faience hen, do you know, Maggie?"

"No, ma'am," said Maggie, and withdrew into the kitchen.

She was not sure that she had done the right thing. Perhaps she should have told Miss Plummer about Mr. Angel and asked her advice. Through the half-open door she could see her moving about, shaking her head in consternation; her house, it seemed to be.

A car was coming now, she heard footsteps on the porch, and before she could reach the door, Miss Dolly had come in followed by Mr. Cassidy with his arms full of packages.

"Oh, Mitzi, you darling!" cried Miss Dolly. "We're late, but we've bought fine things. . . . Excuse us one *minute*, will you?"

She caught sight of Maggie then, and she came toward her and prevented her getting back into the kitchen, and closed the door.

"Maggie," she said. "Come upstairs with me—"

"Miss Dolly, I've got something to tell you—"

"Tell me upstairs. *Please* come along, Maggie!"

Maggie followed her up the narrow stairway to the big room, and Miss Dolly went on into her bedroom.

"I've got a little dress here—" she said.

"Miss Dolly, something's happened."

"Well, what?" asked Miss Dolly bending over her suitcase that was open on the bed.

"Mr. Angel . . . Mr. Angel—met with an accident," said Maggie.

"Oh dear!" said Miss Dolly. "The poor thing told me he wasn't feeling at all well when he was here. Maggie, look! Put this on."

She held up a dress, a new dress she had bought only a few days ago.

"Miss Dolly," said Maggie. "I'm sorry to tell you, but Mr. Angel is dead."

"Oh, heavens!" said Miss Dolly. "I suppose he had a heart attack. I'm terribly sorry. But I've got to speak to you now about this afternoon, Maggie. It's *terribly* important for me."

"Miss Dolly, we'll have to do something about Mr. Angel, first."

"Do something? But, if he's dead—"

"He was—in the river, Miss Dolly; floating away out to sea."

"Maggie! You mean, drowned?"

"No, Miss Dolly. Mr. Curtius found him in the rowboat, dead, and he tipped over the boat. I—think he did that on purpose. I'm quite sure he did. And he wouldn't help me to stop Mr. Angel."

"Stop him?"

"He was—going out to sea," said Maggie swallowing hard.

"I went after him—but I couldn't find him. If we got the police—quick—they could drag the river—"

"Yes, we will," said Miss Dolly. "What a dreadful thing! But now, Maggie, put on this dress will you?"

"What for, Miss Dolly?"

"Maggie, I told you I wanted you here as my secretary. I want to introduce you to these people this afternoon. Put on the dress; it's brand new, and I think it will suit you."

"I'm sorry, Miss Dolly, but I just couldn't," she said.

"Maggie!" cried Miss Dolly. "You can't *possibly* refuse to help me!"

Can't I? thought Maggie.

"Maggie, this is a really important day for me," said Miss Dolly.

An important day for Mr. Angel, too, thought Maggie; but that doesn't seem to bother you much.

"Please remember," said Miss Dolly. "These people are coming here—and I can't let them get the impression that I'm staying alone in the house with two men."

"Well, they'll see me here, ma'am."

"But it isn't the *same*, Maggie! If you're—" She paused, and by the pause, the effort to put the matter tactfully, made it doubly offensive to Maggie. "Anyone can see what an absolutely honest, straightforward girl you are—and if people felt that we're friends—that—that we're confidential together . . ."

"That lady downstairs knows I'm a servant," said Maggie. "I let her in, and I told her my name was Maggie."

"Oh, she doesn't count," said Miss Dolly. "She doesn't notice anything. Oh Maggie, do please hurry up and get ready before the Gettys come!"

"Miss Dolly, something's got to be done about Mr. Angel."

"Of course! I know it. I'll send someone—I'll send Johnny Cassidy to telephone to the police."

"Right away, miss?"

"Yes. The moment I've got you ready."

"I don't need any getting ready, Miss Dolly."

"How *can* you be so stubborn?" said Miss Dolly. "I've tried to be nice to you, Maggie. I asked you to come as a secretary, and you agreed—"

"I can be a secretary, miss, without dressing up in somebody else's clothes—"

"The Gettys will think I'm a bitch," said Miss Dolly.

What a word to call your own self! thought Maggie. But

it impressed her; she felt a reluctant sympathy for Miss
Dolly in this dilemma. Nobody wanted to be talked about,
she thought. I don't think she ever ought to have come here
to this house; but here she is.

"I didn't understand what you meant," she said. "Or I'd
never have come."

"But it's too late now for me to do anything. Maggie,
please . . . !"

"All right, miss," said Maggie. "This once."

It was a lovely dress; Maggie had seen it the day it came
from the shop, and it cost *forty dollars* . . . A sort of long-
waisted effect, and a yoke over the hips and a pleated skirt.

"But my shoes, Miss Dolly. I lost a shoe in the mud—"

"Try these," said Miss Dolly.

Maggie tried on a patent leather pump.

"It's too big for me, miss," she said with quiet satisfaction.

"Well, it's a little too long," said Miss Dolly. "But it's not
too wide. I have very narrow feet."

"Yes, miss," said Maggie. "So have I."

"Well, here, try this," said Miss Dolly, taking off her
suède sandal.

"I guess I can make these do, miss," said Maggie, "if I
fasten the straps in the very last holes."

"Please remember not to call me 'miss.' Call me Dolly."

"I couldn't, miss. I could say Miss Camford."

"All right!" said Miss Dolly with a sigh. "Now let's see . . .
Your hair's perfect. You have very nice hair, Maggie."

"It's naturally curly," said Maggie.

"Here! Here's a new lipstick, Maggie. I'm afraid it's a little
dark, but try it, won't you?"

Maggie made no objection to this. She had never before
used a lipstick, but the idea gave her a small thrill of pleasure.

"Put cold cream on first," said Miss Dolly. "Use plenty of
lipstick, Maggie. . . . No, this way . . ."

Maggie regarded herself in the mirror. She looked taller
in this grey dress, and her face was different; the rich red
lips made her eyes look bluer, and her fair skin, dusted with
powder, seemed dazzlingly fair. I love it, she thought. I'm
going to buy a lipstick for myself.

"Now, let's go down," said Miss Dolly. "And don't open
the door, Maggie. Don't wait on people."

"Who *is* going to wait on the people, Miss Dolly?"

"Not Miss Dolly!"

"Miss Camford."

"We'll all wait on ourselves, Johnny'll mix the cocktails, and I brought along potato chips and popcorn. It's going to be very informal. Let's go down now, Maggie."

"But what about Mr. Angel?" said Maggie with a guilty start.

"Johnny Cassidy will go and telephone."

"But, Miss—Miss Camford, every minute counts."

"It can't if he's dead," said Miss Dolly. "But I'll send Johnny right away.

The doorbell rang.

"Oh, there they are!" said Miss Dolly, catching Maggie by the wrist. *"Please* do the best you can. . . ."

She started down the narrow stairway, and Maggie followed her, suddenly sick with fear. Oh, don't let me make a fool of myself! she prayed in her heart.

Miss Mitzi Plummer had already opened the door, and a man and a woman had entered.

"Gabrielle's pretty shaky," said the man. "It was pretty ghastly. We came over in the launch, you know, and when we went down to the landing-stage, there was a body—a man, washed up on our beach."

It's Mr. Angel, Maggie said to herself. It's a judgment.

SIX

"BUT HOW HORRIBLE!" said Miss Dolly.

"Yes . . ." said Gabrielle.

She was a blonde girl, very thin, with hollows under her cheekbones, and no figure. But she made an asset of her gauntness; she had style, distinction, the fluid grace of a cat, in her plain dark-blue linen dress.

"This is my secretary, Maggie MacGowan, Gabrielle. Maggie—Mrs. Getty. And Mr. Getty."

Maggie did not like the looks of Mr. Getty. He was handsome, in a way, but it was a way too male for her taste, too unromantic. He was dark, stalwart, heavy-shouldered, with a bluish jaw and a quick uncheerful smile.

"How do you do?" he said, appraising Maggie with a quick glance.

"Was it suicide, do you think?" said Miss Plummer.

"Could be, I suppose," said Getty. "But I didn't think of that. Well-dressed fellow, prosperous looking. I thought of murder."

"Murder . . . ?" said Miss Plummer. "But why think of that, Hiram?"

"Well," said Getty, "he wasn't dressed for boating. Didn't look like anyone who'd fallen overboard from any kind of craft. Anyhow, people don't fall overboard in this kind of weather. And suicide didn't come into my head. He was too comfortable looking."

"Strange accidents happen," said Miss Plummer.

"You're right," said Getty. "Anyhow I called up Captain Hofer and he's on the job. We'll soon find out."

"He had white hair . . ." said Gabrielle Getty, unsteadily. "He looked—"

"Take it easy, Gabrielle," said her husband. "Try to forget it. Have a drink."

He looked about the dining-room, and Miss Dolly gave a little start.

"Will you make the cocktails, Hiram?" she asked. "I'll show you where everything is."

He followed her into the kitchen, and Maggie was left along with Miss Plummer and Mrs. Getty. She had grown accustomed to going out of a room when people like these began to talk; she wished with all her heart she could go out now. She sat in a chair, her eyes lowered, she listened to their talk in misery. They talked about art exhibitions, and artists, and people they knew; and what must they be thinking of this Miss MacGowan who had not a word to say for herself?

Johnny Cassidy came in then, and little as she liked him, she had a certain admiration for him, he was so easy, so amiable. He stood beside Miss Plummer, and Maggie heard snatches of this conversation.

"After all," said Johnny, "what is an artist? Dreamer—or maker?"

"A maker, surely," said Miss Plummer.

"But then what of the dreamer?" asked Johnny. "The man with a vision?"

"But the vision must be seized," said Miss Plummer. "As Ruskin says, fine art—ah! Here are the cocktails!"

At the sight of Miss Dolly and Mr. Getty coming in, each with a tray, Maggie rose by impulse.

"Don't get up, Miss MacGowan," said Johnny, and she sat down again.

He came to her in a moment with a cocktail and a glass dish of popcorn.

"Well, thank you . . ." she said. "Only—no, thank you."

He set the glass on the floor, and drew up a chair beside her.

"You ought to be pleased with yourself," he said.

"Why?" she asked, coldly.

"Because you're a very perfect little being," he said. "You always do the right thing."

"Well, I don't," she said.

"You're so nice and neat and pretty," he said. "All one piece. I'd like to be you."

"Well, you wouldn't," she said.

"You sit here," he went on, "despising me."

"I wasn't doing anything of the sort," she said. "I don't despise people, and anyhow I thought the way you were talking was interesting."

"Yes, it was," he said. "I'm a fine talker, very plausible. I can talk in foreign tongues, too. I wonder if you realize what an interesting and colorful personality I am. I've been around. I was in Spain for that show. Camera man. Worked in Paris. Went to Moscow. Do I interest you, Miss MacGowan?"

"Well, yes," said Maggie, considerably at a loss.

He sat down at the floor at her feet.

"I've been around," he said again. "Only now I'm not doing anything, and I don't want to do anything, and I don't like anything. Except you, of course."

He's not joking, exactly, she thought, glancing at his bony face. He looks—I don't know. Kind of queer. Kind of miserable. As if something had gone wrong with him. He's fresh, she thought, there's no doubt about that. But he's—very intelligent. I guess he's the most intelligent person I've ever met.

And here, in this room with Miss Dolly, Miss Plummer, and Mrs. Getty, Johnny Cassidy chose to sit beside Maggie MacGowan.

"Do you write, or anything?" she asked.

"No," he said, "I'm a photographer, same like I told you. I'm trying to get myself sent to China."

"China?" she said with respect.

He looked up at her, his hazel eyes vague and sad.

"Here you see me," he said, "an outcast, a ruined man.

42

Shot to pieces. The Navy turned me down, and the Army. On account of how I've got a bullet in my shoulder."

"A bullet?" said Maggie. "Did you get in in a battle?"

"Oh, yes," he said. "I got it trying to run away from a battle." He rose. "I think I need another drink," he said, and went off to the kitchen.

She missed him. The party had become animated now. Hiram Getty sat on the arm of Miss Dolly's chair talking to her, Miss Plummer sat on the couch beside Mrs. Getty, and Neely, whose entrance she had not noticed, stood before them. Not one of them so much as glanced at Miss Mac-Gowan.

Well, she thought, here I am at a cocktail party. It was not the sort of cocktail party she had seen in the movies, with women in long dresses, and maids and butlers carrying around trays; the background, too, this dusty, untidy dining-room was very inferior. But still, it's interesting, she thought.

She glanced down at the glass that still stood on the floor beside her chair. Well . . . she thought, and picked it up. If I'm at a cocktail party, I'm going to try it.

It was nasty. But there must be something about it, she thought. It must make you feel different. Feel how? One drink couldn't do much harm, when even Miss Plummer had finished her second. I'd sort of like to say that I'd had a cocktail for once, Maggie thought, taking another swallow.

She drank it, all of it, and leaned back to see what would happen.

A car was coming along the road; it stopped, and heavy footsteps mounted to the porch; she rose and went to the door just as the bell rang. It was a square, burly man with a red face, in a uniform. A police uniform.

It's about Mr. Angel! she thought with something like terror. A dreadful, a shocking thing to be sitting here drinking, with Mr. Angel lying dead.

"Mr. Getty here?" asked the man.

"I'll see, sir," she answered. "What name will I say, please?"

He stared at her with his lips pursed, and she realized that Miss MacGowan had spoken like Maggie. But it didn't matter.

"Tell him it's Captain Hofer," said the man, and she went back to the dining-room.

"Mr. Getty," she said, "Captain Hofer's here to see you."

"Come in, Captain!" called Mr. Getty, and rose. "He told

me he'd let me know about this fellow we found on the
beach," he explained to Dolly.

Captain Hofer entered and glanced about the room.

"Good evening, Mr. Getty," he said. "Miss Plummer—
Well, it looks as if the summer had started now all right."

He looked extremely hot; he took out a handkerchief and
wiped his red face. "Whew!" he said. "Now I wonder if
anybody here knows of a Miss Camford—a Miss Dorothy
Camford?"

"That's *meee!*" said Miss Dolly.

"You're Miss Camford . . . ?" He stared at her, pursing his
lips again. "I'm afraid I've got some bad news for you, Miss
Camford. Try to take it easy. You know anybody by the
name of Nicholas Angel?"

"Mr. Angel? Oh yes! He was here to see me this morning,"
she said.

"Now take it easy, Miss Camford," he said. "I'm sorry to
tell you that Mr. Angel has had an accident."

"Oh, poor *thing!* But he told me he wasn't feeling well."

"How did he leave here, Miss Camford?"

"He said he wanted to walk to the station. He said he
thought the exercise would help him. So he started off—"

"Did you notice which way he went?"

"Why no, I didn't," she said. "Is he ill, Captain Hofer?"

"Well . . ." said Captain Hofer. "I'm afraid it's more
serious than that, Miss Camford."

She looked up at him with her dark eyes wide.

"But not—? He's not *dead?*"

"Take it easy, Miss Camford."

Her eyes filled with tears.

"Oh . . . He must have had some sort of heart attack," she
said. "I shouldn't have let him walk."

"Well . . . Maybe not. . . ." said Captain Hofer.

Maggie observed this scene with stupefaction. However
can Miss Dolly be so double-faced? she thought. Tears in her
eyes and all that, when I *told* her long ago about Mr. Angel.
. . . And she's lying. She's lying to the *police.* Well she won't
get away with that. Because *I'm* not going to tell any lies.

The moment Captain Hofer asked her a question, she
would tell him the truth. If that meant trouble for Miss
Dolly and Neely, they deserved it.

"I'm sorry, Miss Camford," said Captain Hofer, "but I'm
afraid I'll have to ask you to come with me, to identify."

"I can't!" she said.

"I'm sorry," he said again, "but I'm afraid you'll have to, Miss Camford."

"I'll go with you, Dolly," said Miss Plummer. "And we can all stop at my house afterwards for a little supper. That'll cheer you up."

"Oh, Captain Hofer, *must* I do this?" asked Miss Dolly.

"Sorry," he said, "just no way out of it, Miss Camford."

She rose and stood holding the back of a chair; Captain Hofer took one arm, and Miss Plummer the other.

"You people follow along," said Miss Plummer. "Somebody drive my car for me, while I go with Dolly. Johnny, won't you? Hiram and Gabrielle can take Neely with them."

She was arranging it all with great gaiety and spirit, making a party of it. "Come Dolly!" she said, and they started, Miss Dolly, white and dazed, like a prisoner between those two. And Maggie let them go. I've got to wait, she thought.

For what she had to tell Captain Hofer was no more or less than an accusation of Neely and of Miss Dolly, and it was impossible to make it publicly in front of all these people. And she did not want to ask Captain Hofer for a word in private either.

Her reluctance surprised her. It's the right thing, to tell him, she thought, and I'm certainly *going* to tell him; only I'd sort of like to warn Miss Dolly and Neely that I'm going to tell. . . . They did not deserve to be warned. The way they were behaving was altogether wrong, and she was certainly in the right about everything. But, standing aside ignored, while these other people made their plans, she felt like a little girl, and to tell Captain Hofer seemed very much like telling tales in school. That was something she never had done.

I'll wait, she thought, till Miss Dolly's identified Mr. Angel. When she comes back, I'll tell her, right out, that Captain Hofer's got to know the whole thing. They were all getting into the cars and driving away; when they had gone she went out on the little porch. A faint mist was rising from the marshes, like smoke; it was not dark yet, but there was no color anywhere. Sad, sort of, she thought.

That Miss Plummer *might* have asked me if I'd like to come to supper. I wouldn't have done it, but she might have asked me. Or Mr. Cassidy or, Mr. Curtius might have said *something*, living right in the same house. . . . I must say it seems a pretty funny way to treat a secretary. A pretty rude way. Sort of—discouraging . . .

A warm indignation began to rise in her, replacing the unwonted melancholy. They had all gone off to supper; let them go. She would get her own supper.

There was nothing to eat; nothing real, no potatoes or vegetables or meat; only a few silly things in cans, shad roe and turtle soup, and fruit salad. There was not even any bread except that rock-like loaf that now had green mould on it. She was hungry, and she was affronted by all of this, by the disorder, the carelessness, by the empty gin bottles and the dirty glasses, the cigarette ashes in the sink. And by this desertion. She went upstairs and it was dark now, she took off Miss Dolly's dress and put on her own black one, and the cap and apron, too. She went down and with tears of wrath, set about cleaning up the kitchen again.

She opened the can of shad roe and fried it, she made tea, and she sat down at the kitchen table and ate. I haven't had a decent meal since I left the city, she thought. I haven't any sheets and blankets, or anything. And then, on top of all *that*, Mr. Curtius has to go and get me to row that boat. . . .

Tears ran down her cheeks. And a cocktail party! she thought. Right after I'd seen—poor Mr. Angel . . . Who ever heard of such a job as this? And what kind of a way to live, with just Miss Dolly and me here with these two men. . . .

The tea did her good, and she went upstairs to get a book. She poured herself out a second cup, good and hot and strong, and just as she prepared to enjoy it, she heard the sound of a motor-boat coming fast. She did not want anybody to see her at her supper in the kitchen; she whisked away her dishes, and stood drinking the hot tea as quickly as she could. The boat was coming into that wooden tunnel now, making waves that dashed against the house, and then the engine was shut off and it was quiet.

It was too quiet. This could not be the party that had left here. No sound of voices, nothing but the wavelets that still lapped against the house. But who would be out there in the dark, in a boat . . . ?

Oh . . . she said to herself, and clapped her hand across her mouth. No! she told herself. I don't believe in things like that. There *aren't*—any ghosts. No. A boat came, and there was—there was a person in it. There had to be. And where was the person now? Sitting out there in the dark? Or lying . . . ?

I just never knew I was like this, she thought. Such a coward. At least I could look out the window . . .

But it was not a sensible thing to go and stand in the lighted window when you did not know what might be outside. She stood very still listening for the sound of a stealthy step on the porch, for a splash in the water; she glanced over her shoulder. If anyone was watching out there in the dark, she must not look frightened, not even hurried.

She set down the teacup and went out of the kitchen, she turned on the light in the dining-room and looked at the stairs. It was dark up there. All right! The more you give in to it, the worse it is. I hate and despise being scared! she said to herself and she started up the stairs. Miss Dolly's sandals were loose on her heels so that they clattered, and if there was anybody else coming up the stairs behind her she could not hear it.

Don't run. And don't turn on the light. She stopped at the top of the stairs and looked down into the lighted hall. There was nothing there. She drew a good long breath and groped her way cautiously into the big sitting-room; she opened one of the windows and stepped out on the balcony.

It was better under the open sky. She stood still, and now she heard voices low voices, but as she drew near the rail they were quite audible.

"But you can get a divorce from a swine like that," said a man's voice, deep, and a little unsteady.

"I know I could, Hiram," said a woman's voice. Miss Dolly's voice. "But—I don't know if I could ever explain—how it is . . ."

"You mean you still care for him?" asked Getty.

"No . . ." Miss Dolly said. "No, it isn't that. It's because he cares so very much for me."

"Is that your idea of 'caring?' " Getty asked. "This damn brute who's made you utterly miserable for years—"

"I knew I couldn't explain," she said with a sort of weariness. "It's really no use. Only, I never really did love him, and he knows that. And it hurts him. . . . I was so young—and so stupid for my age. I didn't know what love was."

"Do you—now?" Getty asked, his voice very unsteady.

"Hiram," she said. "I must go in now."

"No. Wait, Dolly," he said. "Dolly, look here . . . You said . . . You said—let's run away. You said let's go away from the others—"

"I know. It's been a rather dreadful day for me, Hiram, and to-morrow won't be very pleasant. I wanted to go home."

"And you didn't care who came along?" he said. "You didn't want me particularly?"

There was a silence.

"If I did," she said quietly, "it was because when I first met you, I thought you were—rather different from the other men I've met. I thought you'd understand me."

"I *do*," he said after a moment. "You can count on me, Dolly. Always."

So she's married, thought Maggie, overwhelmed.

SEVEN

Miss Dolly came up the stairs slowly; the damp air had made her hair curl at the temples, her damp lashes made her eyes starry. She looked pale, fatigued, very lovely.

"It was horrible, Maggie," she said. "I could never *tell* you how horrible. . . . I didn't like Mr. Angel, I couldn't. But to see him lying there . . ."

She sat down on Maggie's couch, and put her hair back from her forehead. "It seems strange . . ." she said. "I thought I could have a little peace—a little happiness. . . . I need it so. . . . Maggie, do you know why Mr. Angel came here?"

"No, ma'am."

"He came—he's dead now, and I don't want to be bitter—but he came here to ruin everything for me—if he could. You see, an uncle who was very fond of me died last month, and he left me some money; not very much, but enough to give me a little freedom. Mr. Angel was the executor. I asked him for just enough of that money—my own money—to let me get away. But he refused. He said I couldn't have anything for a year at least, until the estate was settled. I couldn't wait a year, Maggie, shut up in that miserable prison of a house."

"Well . . ." said Maggie.

"I borrowed on it," Miss Dolly went on. "It wasn't a good way to do. I knew that well enough. I had to pay an exorbitant interest, and I had to get it from a rather queer man. He makes a business of doing that, advancing money on legacies."

"A *money-lender*, Miss Dolly?" Maggie asked, turning to look at her in dismay. "But, they're terrible! I've known people who got into their hands."

"I know—but I felt—oh, desperate, Maggie. I don't know how Mr. Angel found out about it. He said he was going to tell my uncle and that would have done me a great deal of harm. Maggie, isn't it a strange thing that there are so many people like that? People who can't bear to see anyone else happy."

"Well . . . Yes, ma'am . . ." said Maggie, very doubtfully.

She had been brought up with grave suspicion about happiness; it was a dangerous and frequently a discreditable thing. And to go to money-lenders in order to be happy . . . That shocked Maggie.

What's more, she thought, I didn't hear anything in the beginning about her coming here to be *happy*. She said it was to get away from that man, so that there would not be any scandal. She said it was to translate a book—and what about that? She hasn't been straightforward with me, and I don't like that.

"But, Miss Dolly, I thought you came here to get away from that man," she said.

"I'll never get away from him," said Miss Dolly with sombre despair.

"Well, but Miss Dolly . . ." said Maggie. She paused, embarrassed but resolute. "I don't mean to be prying, but . . . That letter you showed me . . . I mean, it was signed Othello . . . Well, that was Desdomona's husband, wasn't it?"

Miss Dolly glanced at her with dark, blank eyes.

"Yes," she said. "He's my husband."

There was a silence.

"I'll tell you about it," Miss Dolly went on. "I trust you utterly, Maggie. . . . It was years ago in Paris. I went there after my parents died, and I was dreadfully lonely and unhappy. I met this man . . . I needed somebody kind and generous and understanding, and I thought . . . I won't go into all that. Even before we got back from our honeymoon I saw what a ghastly mistake I'd made. I left him and I came home. I didn't tell anyone."

"Not even your aunt and uncle, Miss Dolly?"

"They're the last ones I'd ever tell," she answered, and

was silent again, looking down at her clasped hands. "They'd never understand." She glanced up. "I didn't know what he was like, what a reputation he had. They'd despise me, Maggie. They'd wash their hands of me. And after all—they're all I have. They mustn't know, ever."

She leaned back against the cushions, lost in some melancholy vision, and Maggie looked at her with an uneasy wonder. Here before her very eyes was a woman who had had the tragic experiences that make a heroine, an unhappy marriage, grief, disillusionment; she had lost her home and her money; she was threatened, in danger.

"I suppose this will get into the newspapers," Miss Dolly said. "About poor Mr. Angel. But nobody needs to know anything about the rest of it, anyhow. I mean about his being in the boat."

"But, Miss Dolly, I've got to tell—"

"But why?" asked Miss Dolly. "What earthly difference does it make? It will only make trouble for Neely, serious trouble. The police would *arrest* him, Maggie."

"They'd let him go again if he could prove—"

"There's no reason why he should have to go to court and prove things. He's a genius, I think. It's outrageous to think of his being bullied and tormented for nothing."

"Miss Dolly, I don't think Captain Hofer would bully anyone who was innocent."

"Well, he *isn't* innocent," said Miss Dolly. "I mean I'm perfectly sure it's against the law to move dead bodies. They might be able to send him to prison for having done that. You wouldn't want *that* to happen, would you?"

"Miss Dolly, *I'd* be breaking the law if I didn't tell the police."

"I don't think you would," said Miss Dolly. "I think it's only when you tell the police a lie."

"No, Miss Dolly," said Maggie flatly. "If you know something wrong has been done and you don't report it, that's obstructing the police, and it's being an accessory."

"How can you possibly know all these things?" Miss Dolly asked.

"Because a woman in our street did it. She saw this other woman she knew steal some silk stockings in a department store, and she didn't tell the police. And when they found out that she'd been right there, and must have seen what happened—"

"That's entirely different," said Miss Dolly. "Nobody's

going to find out about this. And if anyone does—very well. Maggie, I'll take the whole responsibility. I'll say I told you not to mention it."

"*Nobody* could tell me what's right for me to do," said Maggie.

They looked at each other straight in the eyes, and they were equally baffled, and equally dismayed.

"You mean you *will* tell? You don't care what trouble and misery you cause for Neely who hasn't done anything wrong?"

"Well, you couldn't call it the right thing to do," said Maggie. "Poor Mr. Angel—"

"He was *dead!*" cried Miss Dolly.

"I know it," said Maggie. "But he shouldn't have been treated *that* way."

They were still looking at each other. Then Miss Dolly sighed.

"I can't argue with you," she said. "You're so obstinate. I'm going."

"Going where, Miss Dolly?"

"I don't know. I don't care. I can't stay here and face this scandal you're going to bring down on my head."

"Well, I can't see how it would be a scandal for you, Miss Dolly. You hadn't anything to do with it."

"Everybody will know why Neely did it. He did it to save me from being worried and harassed. And once that Hofer starts poking into Neely's affairs, he'll find out everything. He'll find out that I took the house for Neely and paid the month's rent."

"Miss Dolly!"

"It's one of the few things in my life I'm proud of," said Miss Dolly. "It's a privilege to help an artist like Neely. But I know very well what Hofer and everybody will make of it. I've been brought up among stuffy, spiteful, self-righteous people. I won't stay here one more minute."

"Miss Dolly! Please tell me where you're going!" Maggie cried.

"I don't know. I'll get a train somewhere. I've got eight hundred dollars in my purse. That'll be enough to take me somewhere—"

Maggie clasped her hands in an unconscious and ancient gesture of despair. She had never before been faced with a moral dilemma; she had not believed that such things existed. Right was right, and wrong was wrong. But not now.

It was plainly her duty to tell the police everything she

knew about poor Mr. Angel. But it was her duty too, to protect another woman from scandal. A scandal it must be. Paying a man's rent was one of the most scandalous things you could do.

No. She could not let Miss Dolly go off alone at this hour of the night with eight hundred dollars in her purse.

"I—I'll try not to tell anyone," she said. "Only if I have to take an oath . . ."

Miss Dolly sat down at the table and began to cry, with her shining dark head on her folded arms. Maggie stood looking down at her in miserable confusion; she had no rules for this. She had heard of, and even known, women who paid a man's rent, but they were not women like Miss Dolly, and they had not acted from any motive like hers. Oh, you wouldn't think that Mr. Curtius would let her! Maggie thought.

Artists are different from other people, so they say. But that Mr. Curtius was young and strong; he *ought* to pay his own rent some way. It isn't right! It isn't! she said to herself. And the way he talked about poor Mr. Angel was horrible, no matter what anyone says.

But she was very sorry for Miss Dolly. Miss Dolly was good in her own way, she had qualms and scruples about that husband of hers; she had spoken to Mr. Getty with an admirable dignity. She was reckless and foolish; but she's a *good woman,* Maggie thought.

And if she had not been a Good Woman in Maggie's own and definite sense, she would have got little sympathy from young Maggie.

Miss Dolly sat up and lit a cigarette; she was pale and tear-stained but calm now.

"It's a miserable beginning for our happy summer, isn't it, Maggie?" she asked.

"Well . . ." said Maggie. She wanted to say that the one to feel sorry for was Mr. Angel, but she was afraid of starting those tears again. Of course, she thought, if Miss Dolly'd seen Mr. Angel the way I did, she'd feel different. That's something to cry about if you like.

Somebody was coming up the steps of the porch; there was the sound of a key in the lock, and in came Neely and Johnny Cassidy.

"The ladies—God bless them!" said Johnny. "And lookie lookie . . . !"

He took a bottle of whiskey out of a paper bag he had

brought in under his arm; he set it on the table and un-screwed the top.

"Glasses!" he said. "Glasses, Neely, for the two lovelies."

Neely shrugged his shoulders in a very foreign way and leaned back against the wall, folding his arms.

"Then I'll get them," said Johnny, moving toward the china closet.

He's drunk, Maggie thought. I hope Miss Dolly'll have the sense to stop him taking any more. But Miss Dolly only sighed.

"I'd be glad of a little drink," she said. "It's been a horrible day."

Maggie hated to see Johnny Cassidy like this, his eyes looking big and starry in his thin face, his dark hair rumpled, a sort of desperate eagerness about him. He doesn't know what he's doing, she thought. Miss Dolly ought to stop him.

"Let's go down to the kitchen, Dolly," he said. "I don't like this room. Let's pretend the kitchen's a bistro in Paris."

She rose, smiling at him. She shouldn't do that, Maggie thought. She shouldn't encourage him to drink any more. She hasn't got much sense, and that's a fact.

"Miss Dolly," she said, "I'm going to bed."

"Oh Maggie! It's early—"

"I'm tired, Miss Dolly. I'm going now. Could you please tell me where I can find some sheets and pillow-cases?"

"Oh, Neely knows," said Miss Dolly. "Tell Maggie, will you Neely?"

"Come!" he said. "Here, this way."

He went into the hall, and Miss Dolly and Johnny Cassidy went down the stairs. There was a narrow cupboard at the head of the stairs, and Neely tried to open it. But the door stuck; he pulled at it, his brows drawn together, a look of leonine ferocity on his face. He gave it a kick and tugged at it, and it came open.

"Take what you want," he said. "There isn't much. But I didn't know she was going to bring another woman."

"You didn't think Miss Dolly'd come here just with you, did you?" asked Maggie indignantly.

"Certainly I did," he said. "Why not?"

"You ought to know better," said Maggie.

"I don't know better," he said. "I suppose they wouldn't let her get away alone."

"Of course she could have come alone, if she wanted to,"

said Maggie, frowning more and more angrily at him. "But she didn't want to. She's not *like* that."

"Like what?" he demanded.

"You know perfectly well what I mean," said Maggie. "She's not *like* that."

"That's silly!" he said. "You talk like a child. How old are you anyhow?"

"That's my business," said Maggie. "Will you kindly move out of the way, and let me see what you've got in there?"

"You're silly!" he said. "You don't know anything of life."

He turned down the stairs, quick and noiseless in his tennis shoes. I could teach *you* a lesson, Maggie said to herself. You rude, nasty-minded beast! Her hands were unsteady with anger as she ransacked the shelves; there was plenty of linen there, or rather cotton, all of poor quality and much of it torn, but at least it seemed to be clean. She took what she needed and closed the cupboard door. Miss Dolly's laugh came to her, clear and gay, very sweet; she heard Cassidy give a shout, then she went into her room and closed the door.

Miss Dolly ought to know better, she thought, while she made up the divan. I'm—well, I'm disappointed in her. She ought to know better than to sit down there drinking whiskey with those two men. And she shouldn't have paid that Neely's rent. He's a sort of foreigner, and of course he takes it the wrong way. Well, if her husband was ever to find out about *this*, he'd have a right to feel jealous.

She turned out the light and lay down. She was tired, very tired, but to her distress, she was not at all sleepy. The water was lapping quietly against the walls, and now and then there was a splash; and what was it that splashed, that jumped out there in the dark?

She thought of Captain Hofer, she thought about Hiram Getty and his wife, about Miss Plummer; she thought about poor Mr. Angel. I just hope there are people who care about him, she thought, people who'll see he has a decent funeral and all.

She had dozed off when the banging of a door startled her wide awake again. I don't know what to make of these people, I really don't, she thought. I'm sorry Miss Dolly's down there drinking. But she's not like Neely thinks. The way she talked to that Mr. Getty was nice.

There had been dignity in that, something sad, and lovely. I liked that, Maggie thought.

Footsteps were coming up the stairs very slowly, they stopped outside her door.

"Good night!" Miss Dolly's voice said, low but always so clear. A man's voice, utterly unintelligible, muttered something.

"Yes, I know that," she said. "I can't get away for ever—not until one of us is *dead*."

The door opened and closed, she crossed the room cautiously in the dark to her own little room, and shut herself in there. And Maggie lay wide awake in the dark for a long time. I suppose that's just a way of talking, she thought. It's hard to tell, with these people, whether they're joking or not.

Only that Neely didn't joke. I wonder, Maggie thought, which one of them she said that to? If Miss Dolly had said that to Johnny Cassidy, it needn't mean anything much. But if she had said it to Neely then it was sort of queer. Sort of worrying.

EIGHT

She waked early, as she had done all her nineteen years, and she got up promptly. And this morning she went to the bathroom in her dressing-gown, she didn't seem to care any more if she met anyone in the hall. She ran a bath, and she did not care whether the noise of the water disturbed anyone. If they waked up, they could go to sleep again. There were no settled hours here, no seemly, pleasant routine.

There was no hot water, and it had to be a bath so cold that it made her gasp. She took her cotton uniform, still wet and muddy from yesterday, down into the kitchen and washed it; in the broom closet she found a piece of rope and she rigged it up on the back porch for a clothes line. She made coffee and drank it, eating a whole box of Kocktail Kracker Bities. There was nothing else.

I'm *hungry,* she thought. The sun was up in the bright sky; it could not be so very early. She got out a broom and a duster, and started on the nasty dirty dining-room; and she felt better with that job of work to do.

The whiskey bottle was empty. Nasty stuff, she thought. Nasty dirty house, and what a way to live. All of them still sleeping, and no breakfast, no decent food . . .

She had such a passion for neatness and cleanliness she was determined to get this disgraceful place in order. And she was determined not to think of anything else just now, not to make any plans, not to look at certain dark unstirring things that were in her mind. Not yet.

A car was coming along the road; she wondered if it could be anything so pleasant and normal as a baker or a grocer. But it was a taxi. It stopped before the house and for a long time she saw a pair of grey gloves moving inside the shadowy interior, then the door opened and Mr. Camford descended.

"What!" he said at the sight of Maggie on the porch.

The taxi drove away and he mounted the steps.

"Kindly tell Miss Camford I'm here," he said.

"Miss Camford's asleep, sir," said Maggie.

"I'm afraid I'll have to disturb her," he said.

He was an enemy. She was clear about that. He looked extraordinarily tall standing on the narrow little porch, he looked curiously distinguished in his grey suit and his grey felt hat, and his grey gloves, and he looked so disagreeable as to be almost funny. Sour-puss, she said to herself.

The miserable embarrassment and constraint she had used to feel in his presence had gone now; she was conscious of her youth, her energy, she felt independent. And she decided not to tell him anything.

He stood there drawing off his gloves and frowning petulantly.

"I've come all this way . . ." he said. "What *is* this place?"

"It's a house, sir," said Maggie.

"Naturally," he said. "But *whose* house?"

"I don't know, sir."

"You must know who lives in it."

She said nothing.

"I don't understand this!" he said angrily. "I was informed last night of poor Angel's shocking accident. Some policeman had found letters addressed to me in his pocket. And this fellow told me that Angel had come out here to see my niece. Who does she know in this place?"

Maggie said nothing.

"I cannot understand this," he said. "Why did you go off like that, without a word to your mistress?"

I haven't any mistress, thought Maggie.

"What are you *doing* here?" he asked, angrier and angrier.

"I'm helping Miss D—Miss Camford," said Maggie.

Holding his grey gloves in one hand he switched at his leg with them.

"I've never heard of such a proceeding!" he said. "It's— What's that?"

It was a voice singing, a rich warm baritone, singing in French something very fancy. It was Mr. Cassidy, Maggie thought.

"What—is—that?" asked Mr. Camford.

"It sounds like the plumber," said Maggie, on the spur of the moment.

For she could not tell Mr. Camford—of all people—anything about this queer household. Miss Dolly could do her own explaining when she came down, and anyhow, thought Maggie, I can't see that it's *his* business. She's a grown woman, and it's her own money.

"Ouvre tes yeux bleus—" Johnny Cassidy sang.

"Oh shut up!" called Neely.

"What's the meaning of *that?*" asked Mr. Camford.

"I don't know," said Maggie.

"I intend to know," said Mr. Camford. "What's more, I intend to put a stop to all this. I intend to take my niece back to New York with me, immediately. Pack her things please, and your own."

"I'm sorry Mr. Camford, but I couldn't do that unless Miss Dolly told me to."

"Er—Annie—Jennie . . ." he said. "You don't understand the situation. Your wages are paid by Mrs. Mayfield and myself, and not by Miss Camford. Miss Camford is not in a position to employ a servant. Now, kindly call Miss Camford, and as soon as she's ready I'll send for a taxi."

"There's no telephone here, Mr. Camford," said Maggie with quiet relish.

"Pshaw!" said he. "Then you can go to a neighbour's and telephone."

"There aren't any neighbours, Mr. Camford."

"Very well!" he said, almost shouting. "I'll get a taxi, somehow. But I want everything packed so that there'll be no delay. I can't afford to waste all day."

"It won't take me long to pack, sir," said Maggie, "if Miss Dolly wants me to do so."

She saw the veins swell in his temples, he slapped the

palm of his hand with his gloves, looking at Maggie, and Maggie at him. *What* a temper, she thought, and her blue eyes were bright with an unholy exhilaration. People in rages made her feel like that. He won't get any change out of *me*, she thought. Let him try!

Then he sighed, and his anger was gone; he took off his hat and smiled ruefully.

"You're quite right," he said. "From your point of view. Naturally—you don't know—you've had no way of knowing, all the complications . . . Suppose we sit down and talk it over?"

"Well . . ." said Maggie.

"Come!" he said. "You sit there, opposite me, and let me explain things to you a little. I think you're going to help me when you understand what I'm trying to do, and that I'm here for no other reason but to help Miss Dolly."

She did sit down then, on the settee opposite him, and it came across her how strange this was. She, in her black dress and Miss Dolly's shoes, sitting here on the porch of a house in the country with Mr. Camford. And he wanted to explain things to her . . . Honestly, she thought, truth is stranger than fiction.

"Miss Dolly's a very impulsive woman," he said. "I dare say you've noticed that. And she's extravagant. Perhaps you've noticed that, too? She's one of those people who have no money sense. It's understandable, heaven knows. She was an only child, you know, and her parents idolized her. Her father left her quite a snug little fortune, not a trust fund unfortunately, but in excellently placed and varied investments. Excellent. She'd have had an income for life, not a spectacular income, but more than adequate. As time goes on, I'm more and more impressed with my brother's good judgment in these investments."

He was silent for a moment, thinking gravely and sadly of those investments.

"It never occurred to me," he went on, "that Dolly would ever attempt to tamper with the financial arrangements her father had made for her. But she did! She went to her lawyer . . . I blame him entirely. He should have let me know at once. But he was an elderly man, and she was an extremely pretty young girl of twenty-three or four."

He smiled, lifting his upper lip and showing a sort of triangle of big even teeth. "That's the way of the world, eh, Jennie?" he said. "He did protest, but not strongly enough.

And she took these gilt-edged securities and sold them and bought—God knows what. She met some fellow who called himself an investment counsellor . . . Well, the long and short of it was that in two or three years' time she didn't have a penny. She came back to us—naturally—and we did what we could to give her a pleasant and normal life. But . . ."

He fell silent, and Maggie waited, a little impressed by this talk of gilt-edged securities and investments. Only I don't see why he's telling *me* all this, she thought.

"We did what we could," he said. "But—as you've seen for yourself, Jennie, we're quiet people, we live quietly, we like the old ways. Dolly wasn't happy. So that when her Aunt Emma left her a few thousands, and she wanted to travel, we offered no objection."

"Well, but—" Maggie began, and stopped abashed.

"Yes?" said Mr. Camford, encouragingly.

"Well, I only meant—nobody could have stopped her, could they, Mr. Camford? I mean, she was grown up and it was her own money . . ."

"That's the crux of the whole matter," said Mr. Camford. "I'm going to explain it to you candidly, Jennie. Once you thoroughly understand the situation, you can be of great help to us—in helping Miss Dolly." He crossed his knees, and leaned his narrow bald head against the wall, looking thoughtfully before him. "You see," he said, "when Miss Dolly came to us after she'd squandered every penny of her inheritance, we found it was necessary to take steps to protect her from her own folly. We knew she'd be coming into more money, later on. So we insisted that everything we did for her was to be called a loan, and that she should sign a note for it. She—as you've no doubt noticed—spends a great deal of money on clothes. Fur coats."

That made him smile again, with that lifting of the lip that made him look rather like an intelligent rabbit.

"She went to Europe," he said. "She spent a year or so in Paris. And she came back penniless, and with a collection of highly undesirable people she called friends. Again she came back to us. Again we had a period of great resentment on her part, and a great many difficulties and sacrifices on our part. We all shared in the distribution of her Aunt Emma's estate, and poor Dolly took an apartment . . ."

He shook his head slowly.

"We needn't go into the details," he said. "She came back

again, and this time she was overwhelmed with debts. She'd even backed some sort of business venture in a shop to sell God knows what from Mexico. Mrs. Mayfield and I paid these debts, and we insisted upon a properly executed note. And now the situation is this. She owes us every penny of this new legacy from her Uncle Paul, and a great deal more. . . . We cannot permit her to squander this . . . For her own sake—and I'll freely admit it—for ours also as well, we *must* put a stop to this."

This was very impressive. It was convincing, too. Everything that Miss Dolly had said and done fitted in with this account. Even the bottle of whiskey. Drink and debts and bad companions . . .

But she was on Miss Dolly's side. She had to be. She had come here with Miss Dolly of her own free will, and she could not go over to Miss Dolly's enemies.

"If you'll go in and pack up her things and your own," said Mr. Camford, "then as soon as Dolly—Miss Dolly is ready, we'll make a start."

"I'll tell Miss Dolly, Mr. Camford," she said.

"Tell her she *must* come with me at once," said Mr. Camford. "Poor Nicholas Angel undoubtedly came out on the same mission—to persuade her to leave this place, whatever it is." He glanced at the front door with a slight frown of suspicion. "In a way," he said, "Dolly's responsible for poor Angel's death—"

"Oh, Mr. Camford!" said Maggie.

"But it's quite true," he said. "He wasn't a young man by any means. And the strain and worry of coming out here so early in the morning . . . What's more, they may have had a stormy interview. No. It may not be pleasant, but it's more than probable that Dolly's directly responsible for Nicholas Angel's death."

He mustn't go around saying that, thought Maggie. That could make things very bad for Miss Dolly.

"She didn't ask him to come, Mr. Camford," she said. "She—didn't want him to come."

"Nevertheless, she was the *cause* of his coming here, getting up early and possibly hurrying to catch a train on a hot morning. He was trying to protect her—as I am. She's very—"

He stopped at the sound of a step on the stairs, and in a moment Miss Dolly came into the dining-room in her wine-red housecoat.

"Uncle Giles!" she cried.

They stood looking at each other with something less than affection.

"Sit down, won't you, Uncle Giles?" she said. "I'll be with you in a moment. Maggie, will you come upstairs please. I want to speak to you."

They went up to Maggie's room.

"Maggie," said Miss Dolly, "has he seen either of the boys yet?"

"No, but he heard them."

"What did he say?"

"Well, when he heard Mr. Cassidy singing, I said it sounded like the plumber."

"Then Maggie, get them away. I'll take Uncle Giles out on the porch. Get them *out* of the house by the back door, and keep them away till he's gone."

"How can I, Miss Dolly? What will I tell them?"

"Oh Maggie, for heaven's sake be a little resourceful. Get them *away!* Maggie, do please try to help me. I've just been through a horrible ordeal—and now there's this other spiteful old killjoy. He's going to talk and talk about how I owe him a million dollars or something. He made me sign all sorts of papers . . . Now hurry, please Maggie!"

"But—" Maggie began, when Cassidy opened his door.

"Hello there!" said Cassidy gaily.

"Hush!" said Miss Dolly. "You must both of you get away from this house, this instant!"

"I want some coffee," said Neely from within.

"Oh, never mind now!" she said. "You'll have to go—"

"No," said Neely. "I want some coffee first. I'll stay in the kitchen with the door shut," he added.

"Johnny," said Miss Dolly, and went to his side. She spoke to him in a whisper, and he listened looking down into her anxious face with a wide grin. Then he beckoned to Maggie.

"Let's gang awa' " he said. "Oot the hoose. Come awa', Neely ma braw—"

"I'm going to make coffee," said Neely.

"All right!" said Johnny. "Come awa', bonnie wee wifie, and we'll find something to eat."

"Go *on*, Maggie!" said Miss Dolly.

"If we want to get away unmarked," said Johnny, "we'll have to go by water. In the rowboat—"

"Oh, no!"

"You can trust me," said Johnny. "I'm a regular little water-baby. Don't be afraid."

But she got into that rowboat with a heart like lead.

NINE

JOHNNY CASSIDY rowed badly, in a one-sided way that made the boat slew round and graze the wall of the boathouse. They came out of that shadow into a steely dazzle, the water glinted everywhere, spread out over the marshes so that it seemed a primeval world without a foothold for a human creature.

He did not go up the creek as Maggie had gone with Neely; he went in the other direction where there were no banks, only the water running among the reeds. This was the route that Mr. Angel must have traveled.

"And that was Dolly's rich bad uncle," said Johnny.

"I wouldn't call him bad," said Maggie.

"All rich people are bad," said Johnny. "But I enjoyed hearing him talk."

"But did you hear him?"

"Every word," said Johnny. "Very interesting it was."

He ran the boat into a jutting clod of earth.

"Maybe I could help you," said Maggie. "I could look ahead and tell you when you're not in midstream."

"That's symbolic," he said. "That's what *you* do. You're always going to stay in midstream, and go right straight ahead. If you hear anyone calling from the rushes, you won't turn your head."

"What makes you think that?" she asked.

"Because you're a virtuous woman," he said, "and they're always deaf and blind. And maybe dumb. I yield to no one in my reverence for virtuous women, but I can't talk to them. Nobody can. Who, I ask you—or rather—to whom do men tell their secrets? They tell them to filles de joie, and to beautiful female spies. Only, not ever to good women in aprons."

The boat ran into the bank with a jar; he pulled away from it, frowning.

"I'll take a turn rowing now, if you like," said Maggie.

His blue shirt was damp with sweat, his hair was damp, his eyes were too brilliant. He's still under the influence of that whiskey, she thought, but not with anger or disgust. She was sorry for him.

"The reason I row like this," he said, "all crooked, is on account of my shoulder."

"Then maybe you shouldn't use it," she said.

"I want to," he said, and she let him alone.

They were coming now in sight of open water.

"Is that the ocean?" she asked.

"The Sound," he said. "There's a place along here where we can get a very fine little lunch. I'm hungry. I don't know why I stay in that damn house with that damn nuisance of a genius. I don't know why I do anything."

He rowed on faster and crookeder, talking in fits and starts, and she was very sorry for him. They came at last to a ramshackle wooden pier over the marsh, and at the end of the boardwalk there was a big wooden house ornamented with fretwork and a cupola. It was a hideous old house, but the scene in general enchanted Maggie; there was a willow tree beside a pond where a flock of ducklings swam, there was a big grey horse looking over a fence.

"It's a real farm," she said.

"You call *this* a farm?" said Johnny, surprised.

"Well, I haven't seen much of the country," said Maggie.

He seemed to know the place well, he led the way into the house to a room in the front shadowed by the verandah, dim and cool and quiet, with five or six little tables covered with white cloths. A stout woman in a very clean white dress, with grey hair screwed into a knob on top of her head, came in from the hall.

"Good morning, Mrs. Albee!" said Johnny.

"Good morning!" said she, severely.

"We'd like a fine fat roast duck—" he said.

"We don't serve dinner till six," said she.

"Make an exception," he said wheedlingly. "I've told Miss MacGowan about your duck dinners, and she's all agog."

"It'll take a good hour and a half," she said, "and it'll cost you a dollar twenty-five cents each."

"So be it," said Johnny.

"No . . . Wait!" said Maggie. "I don't think I can stay so long."

"Sure you can," said Johnny. "It wouldn't matter if you

didn't go back until dinner-time. Or ever. Just sit down and take it a little easy."

"You can sit out on the peeazzer," said Mrs. Albee.

There were some rocking chairs out there, and Johnny dragged one around the corner and set it facing the field where the grey horse stood patiently.

"Now!" he said. "Sit here and look at your farm. Too bad you don't smoke . . . I'll be back presently."

What queer things happen! Maggie thought. If I'd got a job in an office, I'd never have had this experience. . . . Mother was certainly right. You certainly learn more about life this way.

She was glad to sit here and think things over for a while. But, to her distress, her mind was not working with the usual clear energy; a curious haziness had settled upon her. Maybe after a good square meal, she thought . . . and she was shocked to find her mouth literally watering for the roast duck. She had meant to think about Mr. Angel, she tried to, but nothing came of it. Mr. Cassidy's been gone a long time, she remarked to herself.

The horse grazed for a time and then came back to the fence and stood looking at her; she was surprised to see that it had eyelashes, giving it so gentle a look. She could hear a sweet, excited peeping from the little ducks, and after another wait she strolled down to the pond where they went in a proud little flotilla. It was lovely here in the shade of the willow tree, a cat came along and stood for a moment at the edge of the water; then with an absent-minded air, it turned to Maggie and rubbed against her ankles, purring.

Johnny's been gone a *very* long time, Maggie thought. She went back to her rocking chair and waited and waited, and presently Mrs. Albee came out in an apron.

"It's ready," she said.

"Well . . . Do you know where Mr. Cassidy is?" Maggie asked.

"I don't," said Mrs. Albee. "But it's ready, and you better eat."

"Well, I think I'll wait a little while," said Maggie.

She had brought no money with her, and she was not going to start on any dollar twenty-five meal. Where could he be? Mrs. Albee went back into the house, letting the screen door slam behind her; the willow tree rustled and the little ducks peeped.

Restless and growing uneasy now, Maggie went down the

steps again. If the worst comes to the worst, she thought, I'll get in the boat and row home. A picture came into her mind of Mrs. Albee, outraged and justly so, coming after her, calling after her all along the boardwalk. As she set foot on it, she looked ahead to the pier where the boat was tied.

Where the boat had been tied. The boat was not there.

He's gone, she thought. It's one of his mean nasty jokes. He's gone. And she would have to face Mrs. Albee alone. She went back to the rocking chair, sick with dread and dismay. Well, shall I say I'll pay for the dinner later? She thought. Shall I ask her how I can walk home? I just never was in such a miserable position. . . . She'll ask me who I am and where I come from. Well, will I say I'm Miss Camford's secretary? Maybe everyone in the neighbourhood knows about Miss Dolly and me, living in that house with those two men. She'll think . . .

"Hello!" said Johnny coming around the corner.

"Wherever did you go to?" she cried. "Mrs. Albee's got the dinner ready, and I couldn't *find* you."

"I rowed up to the Point," he said, "to see if old Bascom had any clams. Sorry I kept you waiting."

He spoke civilly and nicely and she tried to master her burning desire to go on and on at him.

"I think . . ." she said unsteadily. "I thought—maybe it was a joke. That maybe you thought it was funny to go off and leave me . . ."

"That crazy drunken Irishman," he said.

"I don't mean that," she said. "It's just—"

"Let's eat, Maggie," he said. "You must be hungry, you poor little devil. You must be tired and worried and all upset. You want to go home. Have you got a home?"

"Yes," she answered proudly. "We've got a two family house. Only my mother had to go away."

With his hand on her arm, he steered her toward the front door and into the dining-room. Ms. Albee entered at once with the roast duck beautifully browned, apple sauce, peas, mashed potatoes, spiced peaches, celery.

It was not right to care this much about food.

"God!" said Johnny looking down at his plate.

"What is it?" she asked.

"Ghosts," he said. "Kids in Spain, and old women in China."

She liked him for that. They began to eat, and a strange friendliness was between them. After a while they began

to talk, and it was easy to talk. She told him about her
father and his ship; he told her about his father who had
been a minister in Maine. They ate all Mrs. Albee had
brought them, and when she returned with home-made
strawberry shortcake, they ate that, too.

"It must be terribly late," said Maggie, her conscience
beginning to work again. "Miss Camford will wonder where
on earth I am."

"Why don't you leave here?" Johnny asked.

"Well, why should I?"

"I'd leave if I were you," he said. "I'd leave right now."

"Well, why?"

"Oh, there are things going on," he said. "Things are
going to happen."

"What kind of things?"

"Things you won't like," he said.

"That can't be helped," said Maggie, and there was a
silence between them.

"I'd like to row back," said Maggie presently, and Johnny
consented.

He was peaceable now, he sat facing her, his big thin
hands clasped between his knees, a mild and thoughtful
look on his face. She felt peaceable too, and contented. The
sun was low, and she took it easy, rowing with a leisurely
rhythm against the current that was surprisingly strong.

"The tide's going out," she said.

"So it is," said Johnny. "Going fast. And the sands of
life . . . Oh Lord! If I could only get away. If I could only
get back to a war!"

"I can't understand that," said Maggie with a certain
severity.

"No," he said, "I don't think you could. That's because
you have no craziness in you. I'll explain." He took out a
cigarette and lit it. "War is the grand supreme simplifica-
tion. You have the Good People banded together, all very
cosy; and you have the Bad People. The Enemy. When I'm
not in wars, I have a lot of trouble telling the good people
from the bad. I have a lot of trouble knowing what to do. Or
wanting to do anything. You don't have these worries in a
war."

She had never before met anybody like Johnny Cassidy,
and the people in the stories she had read, and the movies
she had seen were not like this. Yet she felt curiously at ease
with him. She could talk to him, perhaps because *he* could

66

talk; he was able to say all the things that came into his head. He was silent now for a time and she wondered what he was thinking about, and what had happened to make him like this.

"I'd like to ask you a favor, Miss MacGowan," he said with courteous formality.

"Yes," she said seriously.

"If you didn't mind," he said, "I'd like to touch your hair when the sun shines on it. I'd like to lay my hand on it."

The color rose in her cheeks. She was profoundly embarrassed. He leaned forward and put his hand on the crown of her head for a moment and then sat back.

"It's warm!" he said. "It's alive. You're alive, you little healthy thing . . ." He sighed. "You'll take my advice, won't you, Maggie and leave here? Go this afternoon."

"I couldn't leave Miss Dolly like that."

"If you're short of money—"

"I'm not, thank you."

"If you're worried about finding another job—"

"I'm not, thank you."

"Then why d'you stay?" he demanded. "There's nothing here for you. Go away, won't you Maggie? Please! I'll drive you to the station."

"I couldn't go like that," she said. "I'd have to talk it over with Miss Dolly."

"I tell you there's trouble coming."

"That's all the more reason why I couldn't just walk out on her," said Maggie briefly.

They had now reached the entrance to the boathouse, and she rowed into that darkness. Johnny Cassidy got out and held out both his hands to her; he made the boat fast, and they walked in silence to the door of the kitchen. There was a sound of voices, a man talking,

"My goodness!" said Maggie. "D'you suppose Mr. Camford's still here?"

"That's not Camford," said Johnny. "That's Hiram Getty."

He and Miss Dolly were in the dining-room, and the only way for Maggie to avoid them was to remain in the kitchen. And she wanted to avoid them, for some reason she did not trouble to analyse. She sat down in a chair and surveyed the kitchen.

It was like a nightmare. No matter what she did to it, no matter how she left it, it was always like this when she re-entered it; dirty dishes and glasses, and pots and pans, a demoralized look about it.

"Well . . ." said Johnny and opened the door; he went into the dining-room and closed the door after him.

Of course, I'm not going to stay much longer anyhow, she thought. But I'll give Miss Dolly time to find somebody else, another secretary. She certainly couldn't stay in this house here with these two men. Well, maybe Mr. Camford persuaded her. Maybe she'll be going home herself. She ought to. She wouldn't have to be so miserable back in their house. She could have a nice life there. She could have nice friends. She could do something. She could do war work or something for charity. If she owes all that money—

"Oh, Maggie," said Miss Dolly pushing open the door. "You're back . . . ?"

"Yes, Miss Dolly. Is—Mr. Camford upstairs?"

"No, he gone," said Miss Dolly. "Will you make cocktails please, Maggie?"

"I don't know anything about making cocktails, Miss Dolly," said Maggie.

"I'll teach you," said Getty, standing behind Miss Dolly.

Maggie was about to refuse to learn, but she changed her mind. It's just as well to know how to do things, she thought. You never know. So she listened to Hiram Getty with attention; under his direction she measured out gin and vermouth, bitters and lemon juice into a glass jug. She put in ice cubes and stirred it all with a wooden spoon.

She memorized the formula, and she felt a little pleased, a little proud; it was, she thought, sort of sophisticated. But she would not take a drink, even a sip.

"No thank you, Mr. Getty."

"You've never tried one, Maggie," said Miss Dolly.

"Excuse me, but I have, Miss Camford," said Maggie.

Johnny was coming down the stairs now, his face bright at the sight of the jug on the dining-room table. Liquor's a *hateful* thing! Maggie thought, and went upstairs to get away from it.

The door of Neely's room was half open, and on the drawing-board she caught sight of a little landscape in watercolors, so vivid it looked that she stopped, fascinated. The room was in wild disorder; on the deal table were paint and brushes and crayons. There were clothes all over the room, and there were two canvas cots unmade. I suppose

Johnny sleeps in here too, she thought. There doesn't seem to be any other room.

She wanted a better look at the little picture, and she went in. It was just a bit of marsh, the green reeds and the brown creek; strange that he could so infuse it with light. He had made it *his* marsh, you recognized it, but only he could see it like this.

Maybe he was a genius. If so, she might make up his cot for him, and Johnny's, too. She turned to cross the room when she saw something that astounded her. On the seat of a chair she saw a wallet that she knew very well. It was a pigskin wallet with the initials G.C.C. in a corner. It was Mr. Camford's wallet, and it was soaking wet; there was a little pool of water under the chair.

She backed away from this and out of the room; she closed the door and leaned against the wall.

What does it mean . . . ? What does it mean . . . ? she said to herself.

She remembered Mr. Camford telephoning home once from his office, with orders for her to look under his pillow for that wallet. He thought a lot of it; he kept important things in it— What does this *mean* . . . ?

TEN

THEY WERE laughing downstairs, all very lively, Miss Dolly and those three men. Maggie stood at the head of the stairs, listening to them, and she was completely at a loss. Something had to be done about Mr. Camford's wallet; somebody had to be told. And there was nobody here that she trusted.

It startled her to realize that. Not one of them, she thought. Not the Gettys, and not Miss Plummer, certainly not Neely. And not even Miss Dolly. She doesn't tell the truth, and she's not sensible about things.

Well, Mr. Cassidy? she thought. She considered him for a moment, and then ruled him out. I don't really know how he feels about things, she thought. I wish I could have a talk with Mother. Or Mrs. Crabtree.

Mrs. Crabtree! She nearly said the name aloud. But that's the thing to do, she cried to herself. I'll call up Mrs. Crabtree, and find out if Mr. Camford's come home. If he has, then everything's all right. And if he hasn't, I'll tell *her* about the wallet, and she can tell Mrs. Mayfield.

She went down the stairs then greatly fortified by this plan of action. If there's been any monkey business, she thought, if anyone's tried to rob Mr. Canford, they're not going to get away with it.

She entered upon a strange and disturbing scene. Miss Dolly sat with her arms stretched out on the dining-room table, holding a glass; Hiram Getty stood beside her, and she was looking up at him with a sweet drowsy smile; Johnny Cassidy sat opposite her staring fixedly at her, Neely stood leaning against the wall with his arms folded. They didn't look like nice, well-bred people, any of them, in that dirty, disorderly room, they too looked disorderly and queer.

"Have a drink, my pretty pigeon," said Johnny Cassidy.

"No, thank you," said Maggie. "I don't drink."

"You can learn, dear, if you try," said Johnny gently.

Maggie did not answer. He's drunk, she thought. *He* couldn't drive me to where I could telephone to Mrs. Crabtree. He was the one she had meant to ask; now it would have to be either Hiram Getty or Neely. And it was hard to think of a way to approach either of them. I can't tell them what I want to do, she thought, because—

Because somebody in this room knew about the wallet; somebody had put it where she had found it. Maybe more than one person knew, maybe they *all* know. I don't really understand any of these people, she thought. I don't know what's going on.

Johnny sat down again and took up his glass.

"I died—three years ago—in Paris," he said in the same gentle tone, looking before him at nothing. "Did you know that, Getty?"

"No," said Getty, curtly.

"Now, you, for example," said Johnny, "you've never been alive at all. You—"

"Johnny, don't be silly," said Miss Dolly.

"Why not, dear?" he asked. "Here we are, all riding on a merry-go-round, on dragons and horses, and it's very silly. I thought once that I was riding on a horse with wings, but the wings fell off, and the horse never got anywhere. Just went round and round. We're all going round and round . . . And there's good, *good* little Maggie watching us, all aflame with virtuous indignation."

"Johnny, you've had too much," said Miss Dolly.

"You're right, dear," he said. "I've had too much of everything. Too much love, too much joy, and I am sick of an old pain. I have been faithful to thee—Cyn—"

"Hiram, let's go up and sit on the balcony," said Miss Dolly, rising.

"Whither thou goest, there go I," said Johnny, getting up, too. "And who knows? Maybe Getty and I, locked in a death-struggle, will both fall off into the water and drift away locked in each other's arms."

"Johnny, lie down and go to sleep for a while," said Miss Dolly.

"I might have a nightmare," he said.

"Come, Dolly!" said Getty, taking her arm. "This is—"

"Sickening," said Johnny. "Sickening."

He picked up the whiskey bottle by the neck and followed the other two out of the room; he began to sing in his fine tenor voice.

"Ridi! Pagliacci . . ."

Neely still leaned against the wall with his arms folded. Well, is he drunk, too? Maggie thought, and she decided to get him talking, so that she could find out about that. Only it's so difficult to begin.

"Why do you stay here?" he said so abruptly that she started.

"Because it suits me," she said.

"You don't like any of the people here," said Neely, "and they don't like you. Why don't you go away?"

"You're polite, aren't you?" said Maggie.

I don't care about being polite," he said. "Why don't you go away and do something useful? Some war-work, go and do."

"Well, why don't *you?*" she said.

"I'm going all right," he said. "Once they make up their minds whether they'll take me in the Army or send me to Ellis Island as a dangerous enemy alien."

In spite of her indignation against his rudeness, she was interested.

"I thought Dutch people were all right," she said.

"Certainly they're all right," he said. "Only they can't make up their minds if I'm Dutch or not. I think I was born in Berlin."

"Don't you *know* where you were born?"

"No. Who does? You know that somebody tells you, that's all. Very well. I think my mother told me I was born in Berlin. I think she brought me to this country on the German quota. But I don't know what her name was."

"You don't know your own mother's name?"

"No," he said. "That's the way the Immigration people talk to me, and the Army people, and the police. Even someone from the F. B. I. They think I'm very fishy. Well, I don't care. In the meantime I can go on with my work."

"But I don't see how you can not know your mother's name," said Maggie.

"For this reason," he said, with an impatient frown. "My father was—I don't know—something bad. A drunkard maybe. Anyhow my mother left him, and she took back her maiden name. I don't know if she got a divorce, or if she just went away. Anyhow, she brought me over here. She said we would use the name of her family, Curtius, and what did I care? I was only a child. Well, I think we had a different name on the passport, and I don't remember what it was. So they can't find any record of how I got into this country, and that makes them mad. I don't care about that, either."

He was rude and curt, and queer, but she did not think he was drunk.

"Mr. Curtius," she said resolutely, "will you please drive me to some place where I can telephone?"

"Why?" he asked.

"Well, because I want to make a call," she said.

"Who is it you want to call?"

"Well, really . . ." she said. "I think that's my own affair."

"I think I won't drive you anywhere," he said.

"But why?" she said, startled.

"Because you want to make trouble," he said. "Because you're a little spy."

"*What?*"

"That's it," he said. "I know—"

He stopped and turned his head, listening to a car that was coming up to the house.

"Now, if it's that damn policeman . . ." he said. "I'll do the talking."

But it was Miss Mitzi Plummer.

"Neely-boy!" she cried.

"What do you want?" he said.

"But aren't you going to let me in, Neely?"

"I don't care if you come in or not," he said, and in a moment she appeared in the dining-room doorway.

"Oh, it's you?" she said, eagerly, glancing at Maggie. She sat down in a chair looking immense and curiously formal in a black silk dress and a silver turban. "Neely!" she said.

"Yes?" he shouted from outside.

"But come here, my child!" she said. "Willie Hofer's been at me and at me—about *you*."

He came back into the dining-room.

"All right!" he said. "You don't know anything about me. Tell him that."

"He asked me," she said, and began to laugh, "he asked me what were the relations—between you and Dolly."

"Shut up!" said Neely, and turned on his heel and went away.

"Neely, come back!" she cried. "I won't tease you any more. I came to bring you home to dinner, Neely. I've got such a *nice* chicken—"

The screen door slammed and he was gone.

"He's a fascinating boy," said Miss Plummer. "But, of course, I'm quite definitely masochistic."

"What's that?" asked Maggie.

"I like to be ill-treated," said Miss Plummer. She smiled dreamily. "I'd love to be tortured," she said.

Maggie looked at her with disgust, and a dim fear. This was something new to her and it was bad.

"Does that shock you?" asked Miss Plummer.

"Well . . ." said Maggie.

"Tell me, child, where do you come from?"

"From Brooklyn," said Maggie.

It nettled her to see Miss Plummer laugh at that.

"Really," said Miss Plummer, "you're the most macabre little note, my dear, in a very gruesome set-up. This is my house, you know, and Dolly rented it from me for the summer—for a marvelous genius, she *said*. Of course I came to call on him the moment he arrived, and I adored him. There he was, painting away, with nothing to eat in the house. Can't you picture him jumping into the water and catching fish in his hands, and eating them raw?"

"No," said Maggie.

"I can. *I* think he's divinely savage. But then—along came Johnny, and I can't cope with him. I called up Dolly, and she told me to let him live in the house, too. That did seem unnecessarily depraved, but, after all, it's not *my* affair. Is it?"

"No . . ." said Maggie trying to understand the implication of all this.

"Now, I'm simply waiting," said Miss Plummer. "It's fascinating. I'm simply waiting—for the murder."

"*What* murder?" said Maggie.

"I *hope* it will be Dolly," said Miss Plummer. "But maybe that's too obvious. Well . . . !" She rose. "I'll be running along now. Would *you* like to come back to dinner with me, you quaint child?"

"No, thank you," said Maggie. "But—if you'd drive me some place where I could telephone, Miss Plummer—"

"Why not?" said Miss Plummer. "Come along!"

Maggie hesitated for a moment. She was not in the habit of walking out of a house without a word; her mother had always expected to be told where she was going and when she was coming back, and Mrs. Crabtree had been like that, too.

But no, she thought, I'm not going to tell Miss Dolly. I'll be back in time for dinner. I'm not going to be polite and considerate in *this* house.

It gave her a certain pleasure to walk off like this. Only I don't like Miss Plummer, she said to herself. I think she's awful. Is she crazy, I wonder? She glanced at Miss Plummer, starting her little car, at her face with the heavy-lidded eyes, the bold nose, the full lips, the double chin. You can't tell by looks. But the things she said . . . Waiting for the murder?

The sun was in the west, and the summer world was very tranquil. They left the house and the marshes behind and came to the highway where there were other cars and trucks, and a bus.

"If you'll just leave me at the nearest place where there's a telephone, please, Miss Plummer."

"Yes, yes," said Miss Plummer. "You know, I thought this Mr. Angel had been murdered, but Willie Hofer says definitely, no. Natural causes. A stroke of some sort. Willie's theory is that Mr. Angel was walking along by the creek, and fell in. He wasn't drowned; they can tell, you know. I said to Willie, but *why* should he be walking around alone in that godforsaken landscape? And Willie gave me a piercing, sleuthish look and said—how do you know he was alone? Willie's not stupid."

Well, if he wasn't drowned, and wasn't murdered, Maggie, thought, it can't make any real difference for Captain Hofer not to know about Mr. Angel in the rowboat. But I wish he

74

did know. I wish I'd told him right away. I think I made a mistake, not to tell him.

I think I made a mistake to come here at all. I think I've got into something that's sort of out of my depth . . . I think . . . The conclusion she was reaching was so novel, so very unpleasing that she balked at it. But in the end, she took the hurdle. I guess I'm not as smart as I thought I was, she said to herself.

"Well, here we are!" said Miss Plummer.

She stopped the car before a shabby little house with a garden surrounded by a picket fence, in a street of other little houses like it; as they got out, a train went roaring past along the tracks at the corner.

"My father's mill hands used to live here," said Miss Plummer. "I used to walk by here sometimes with my governess, and wonder what sort of animals they were. Now the wheel has turned, and here I am myself."

The door of the house was not locked, she opened it and Maggie followed her into a little hall where a large oil-painting hung, hot with color. "There's the telephone in the sitting-room," said Miss Plummer. "I'll go and get us a drink."

Maggie sat down at the desk and got long distance on the old-fashioned telephone; while she waited for the Camford number to answer, she looked about her, and she was impressed. It was a small room, crowded and dusty, but it was a room of great culture, bookshelves on three sides, paintings on the walls, and statues standing about. I'd like to know more about Art, she thought. I've got a lot to learn.

"Hello!" said a familiar voice that made her heart leap.

"Oh . . . Mrs. Crabtree?" she said. "This is Maggie."

"*Well!*" said Mrs. Crabtree. "I must say I'm surprised to hear from *you.*"

"I know," said Maggie. "I'll explain it all some day, Mrs. Crabtree. Only just now, I'd like to know . . . Mrs. Crabtree, is Mr. Camford home yet?"

"No," said Mrs. Crabtree, "he's not."

"Well . . . Are you expecting him, Mrs. Crabtree?"

"No," said Mrs. Crabtree. "We are not."

"Mrs. Crabtree, I'm *worried* about Mr. Camford."

"*Indeed?*" said Mrs. Crabtree.

"I am! Really I am! I can't tell you now—but I think I'd better speak to Mrs. Mayfield."

"If you're really worried," said Mrs. Crabtree, relenting a

little, "then I don't mind telling you we had a wire from him not long ago. He's gone to Boston."

"A wire? A telegram? What did it say, Mrs. Crabtree?"

"It said he'd gone to Boston."

"But—"

Miss Plummer took the receiver out of her hand and pushed her aside so roughly that she nearly fell off the chair.

"Time's up," she said into the mouthpiece. "Good bye!"

She hung up, and turned to Maggie.

"What's all this about?" she asked.

"It's—a private call," said Maggie.

"You're trying to make trouble, you red-headed little hellion," said Miss Plummer. "Come on!"

"Come—where?"

"I'm going to take you back to the boathouse," said Miss Plummer. "And this time you'll stay there. Come on!"

"I'll go home by myself."

"Oh, no you won't. You're not going to go wandering around telephoning to people and making trouble. Who are you, anyhow, and where did Dolly pick you up? Come along!"

"I won't!" said Maggie.

"All right!" said Miss Plummer. "I'm not going to make a scene now in broad daylight and drag you out. You'll stay here then until it's dark."

"I won't!" said Maggie.

"Just try to leave," said Miss Plummer.

It was a well-populated street with houses on either side of this and all the windows were open, a cry for help would surely be heard. But you can't just begin to yell, Maggie thought, when you haven't been hurt or anything.

"You're a nasty little thing," said Miss Plummer. "I thought so the first time I saw you. A smug, self-righteous, common little thing . . ."

Was that how she seemed to these people? Was that what she *was?*

No! she said to herself. And aloud, "I've got p-plenty to say for myself," she retorted.

"Then say it. Who were you telephoning to about a telegram?"

"That's my business," said Maggie.

"I'll find out," said Miss Plummer. "You don't imagine you're a match for *me*, do you, brat?"

Maggie did not answer. She stood looking down at the

carpet that glowed in deep blue and ruby red in a bar of sunlight. She was wounded, stricken by these words. She thought of herself at the cocktail party in Miss Dolly's dress— and this was how she had seemed? She thought of the duck farm and the nice things Johnny Cassidy had said to her. I suppose he was sorry for me, she thought. I suppose that's how people felt about me when I was looking for a job.

"Come into the kitchen," said Miss Plummer. "I want a drink."

She was breathing faster, color had risen in her swarthy face, her mouth was set in an ugly line. She's working herself up into a regular rage, Maggie thought, alarmed.

"I *said*, come into the kitchen!" said Miss Plummer.

It's broad daylight and there are plenty of people around, Maggie thought. There isn't really anything to be frightened of.

But she was frightened. A train was thundering along, and the house shook, the windows rattled; the sunny little room seemed suddenly hot beyond bearing. I can just walk out, she told herself. But she did not believe that. She thought Miss Plummer would pounce on her like a cat if she moved. And Miss Plummer looked so big, so heavy, so powerful.

"No," said Maggie, "I won't go in the kitchen."

"You—" Miss Plummer began, her eyes narrowed.

The front door opened and Johnny's voice called.

"Whaur's ma wee lassie?"

ELEVEN

"Wait!" said Miss Plummer, and as he appeared in the doorway she put her hand against his chest, and pushed him out into the hall. They began to talk in low voices.

Maggie crossed the room to a mirror hanging against the all. Well, anyhow, I look neat and clean, she said to herself with a sob rising in her throat. Anyhow, I don't drink and carry on like these people.

But this gave her little comfort. She had lost the regard of everyone, above all, of Mrs. Crabtree. If my mother were here, she thought, I'd go right straight back to her now. I'd learn more about life in a position like this, Mother said. Well, I certainly have. I've learned enough to last me for a long time. . . .

Miss Plummer came back into the room now followed by Johnny.

"I came to take you home, dear," he said gently. "Ready?"

His eyes were soft and starry in his white face; he swayed on his feet as he spoke to her.

"But—you're not going to drive, are you Mr. Cassidy?" she asked.

"I can drive anything—any time," he said. "You're safe with me."

"Thank you, but—"

"Oh, go along!" said Miss Plummer. "You can't stay here."

"I can take a taxi."

"Come with me, Maggie," said Johnny.

"Don't be such a snivelling little coward," said Miss Plummer. "Go on! Get out of my house!"

She made a sort of rush at Maggie, and Maggie stepped back into the hall.

"Go on! Go on! Go on!" cried Miss Plummer, flapping her hands at Maggie. Johnny opened the front door and Maggie went out on the veranda.

"Go on! Go on!" cried Miss Plummer, coming out after her.

There was something so confusing, so alarming in the clamor she made, in her flapping hands, in her looks, so big in her black satin . . . Maggie got into the car with Johnny.

"Drive fast!" screeched Miss Plummer from the top of the steps. "It's much easier that way, Johnny. Drive fast! Drive like hell!"

"Don't you do it," said Maggie. "She's—she's a dreadful woman."

"I'll be careful, dear," said Johnny.

He did better than she had expected; he drove steadily enough back to the highway and along it, and then he turned into a side road.

"Is this—? Are you sure this is the right way?" she asked.

"I'm headin' south," he said. "Let's get away from all this. I've got to get away. Let's go down to Mexico."

She felt like crying in her fatigue and wretchedness. But he would have to be managed.

"I've got to get my things first," she said. "Let's go back—"

"No going back," he said. "Time marches on. And you

haven't any 'things,' poor pretty little Maggie. Just scraps and odds and ends."

She was crying now.

"They're things—I want, anyhow. Please let's go back."

"I'll buy you things," he said. "I'll pull myself together and start a new life, with you. I'll be good because you're so good."

"Please, Johnny . . . I couldn't leave Miss Dolly like this—"

"*I* could," he said. "*She* thinks I can't get away. But she's wrong. She thinks she's put a spell on me. She thinks— Did you ever read about Paolo and Francesca, Maggie machree?"

"No, I never did."

"They went round and round in hell, in each other's arms. Round and round and round—"

He ran the car up on a bank with a jolt that made her feel faint.

"I'm *sorry!*" he said seriously. "But now that we're here, let's stay. Will you let me sleep a little while with my head in your lap, my sweet? For I am weary and I fain would rest."

"Let's just stop at the house first, Johnny."

"You're a guileful little dove. Oh Maggie, Maggie! If I could sleep with your hand on my brow, I'd wake up cleansed and new."

He closed his eyes and held her hand against them.

"Johnny dear . . ." she said. "I'm so tired—and my head aches. Will you *please*—take me home?"

"Oh God!" he said. "Poor little Maggie . . ."

"*Come* on, Johnny. It's getting so late. Look at the sun . . . Johnny, please . . ."

She got him to start the car again but he would not turn back to the highway.

"Where does this road go?" she asked him.

"Who knows?" he said sadly.

It was little more than a lane, and completely deserted. He drove slowly, jolting over ruts and stones, there were fields on either side and the grain rustled in the light breeze. The sun was gone, leaving a light that was pallid and clear. Around a bend in the lane they came into woodland, and it was dark here, the trees almost meeting overhead, and the branches brushing lightly against the top.

Maggie was not frightened any more, not angry at Johnny,

not even impatient. He's in a miserable state, she thought, and she meant that in more ways than one. She had always despised drunkenness, but she was not despising Johnny now. She was dreadfully, unbearably sorry for him. He's—sort of lost, she thought. What makes people do things like that? Things like drinking—or worse . . . And then there are the other people like Father and Mother, like Mrs. Crabtree— they don't even *want* to do anything bad . . .

He drove on and on along the winding lane under the shade of the trees. And she didn't care much anymore where they were going. I'll telephone to Mrs. Crabtree again to-morrow, she thought. I'll find out where Mr. Camford went in Boston, and then I'll find out if he ever got there.

Ever got there . . . ? That sounds—queer. He does go to Boston every now and then. He could have dropped his wallet somewhere and not missed it until he got on the train. Well, maybe he was in too much of a hurry to come back for it. Maybe there's nothing at all to worry about.

Anyhow, what *am* I worrying about? Mr. Angel had a stroke. Well, the same thing wouldn't happen to Mr. Camford, too. That would be too much of a coincidence. Nobody really did anything to Mr. Angel. There's no reason to think anything—anything terrible has happened to Mr. Camford.

Only I do feel worried. I do! If I only knew he was safe in Boston . . . I'll have to find that out. I'll have to do some-thing about it. And the definite purpose discouraged her. She did not feel smart and sure any more.

The moon was up and shining through a silver mist when they turned into the road that led to the boathouse. How lonely the lighted windows looked! How lonely the world was . . . Johnny stopped the car and got out; he held out his hand to Maggie, and when she took it, it was cold and damp. Poor Johnny . . .

He stumbled going up the steps, and fell, and she helped him up. "I'm sorry . . ." he said.

"That's all right, Johnny," she said.

She opened the door, still holding his arm, and they entered the hall. He looked as white as a ghost, blinking his eyes in the light; he looked so forlorn.

"Need a drink," he said.

"No, you don't, Johnny," she said. "You'd better go right straight to bed."

"Maybe so," he said. "Good night, dear."

She stood watching him while he climbed the stairs, and she turned toward the kitchen. I'll make a cup of tea, she thought. That'll do me good. I haven't had a bite since lunch. Lunch at the duck farm, and was that only to-day? I do wish I knew the time.

She pushed open the swing door, and stopped short, astounded at what she saw. Neely in singlet and flannel trousers, ironing. He had the folding board set up, he had a wicker basket of clothes on a chair beside him, and he was working in a methodical and matter-of-fact way.

"Hello!" he said, glancing at her.

"Hello!" she answered and drew nearer.

He stood the iron on end, and smiled at her.

"Now will you finish this?" he asked.

"Finish your ironing?" she said. "And why should I?"

"You're a girl," he said. "You know about things like this."

"I'm going to make some tea," said Maggie. "I'm tired."

Neely sat down on the edge of the table and lit a cigarette.

"I never tried to iron before," he said. "Only if we're going away to-morrow—"

"Who? Who's going where?"

"We're all going, you too, on Getty's yacht. We're going to take a little cruise up to Maine."

Maggie put on the kettle, and began to look for something to eat. I'm not going on any yacht, she said to herself. "You'd better disconnect that iron," she said. "It's just wasting current."

He rose at once, and unplugged it.

"I'll be glad to go on the cruise," he said. "See something new. Will you like it?"

"No," said Maggie, taking butter and two eggs out of the ice-box.

"You're quick," said Neely. "I like that. I think you're very clean, too."

"Certainly I am," said Maggie.

"Have you a lover?"

"What do you mean?"

"A lover—a sweetheart."

"No," said Maggie, "and I don't want one either."

"That's silly," said Neely. "When you've had your supper, will you finish this ironing for me?"

"No," said Maggie again.

"I want to look nice," he said. "They're very rich, these Gettys. They could help me a lot."

81

She fried the eggs and made a pot of tea, and carried the tray into the dining-room.

"Why do you go away?" asked Neely coming after her.

"Because I don't want to quarrel with you," said Maggie.

"I don't mind if you quarrel with me," he said.

"Well, I do," she said, and he walked off to the kitchen.

When she had finished her inadequate supper, she left the dishes where they were; what did it matter in this house? She was tired, very tired, and she was going to bed. But when she opened the door of her room she found Miss Dolly in there, kneeling on the floor in her housecoat, packing a suitcase, a cigarette between her lips.

"Oh, Maggie!" she said. "I thought you'd *never* come."

"I'm sorry," said Maggie, unconvincingly.

"We're leaving to-morrow, Maggie—"

"Well, not me, Miss Dolly. I'm sorry, but I'm not going on this yacht."

Miss Dolly looked at her with dismay in her dark eyes.

"But Maggie, it's going to be lovely. A cruise—"

"I'm sorry, Miss Dolly. But I thought I was going to be your secretary—"

"But I'm going to begin working on the book, Maggie. I'll start when we get on the yacht."

"I just can't do it, Miss Dolly."

Maggie sat down on the bed, and Miss Dolly sat back on her heels.

"Miss Dolly." Maggie said, "I'm worried about Mr. Camford."

"Please!" said Miss Dolly. "Please don't *mention* him, Maggie. You don't *know* how horrible he was to me this morning."

"Well, I'm worried about him," said Maggie, doggedly.

"By why should you be? He's gone—"

"Miss Dolly, did he say where he was going?"

"He said something about going to Boston. But—we had a quarrel, Maggie. He was horrible to me—he said horrible things."

"Did he go away in a taxi, Miss Dolly?"

"Oh, I don't *know!* I left him. I went out of the house and left him here."

"Miss Dolly . . ." Maggie paused a moment, curiously reluctant to go on. "Did you leave him alone in the house?"

"Yes," said Miss Dolly, her eyes fixed on Maggie's face. Then a change like a shadow came across her face. "Yes . . .

I think so . . ." she said. "I'm pretty sure, Maggie. Why do you ask, Maggie?"

"I've got my reasons, Miss Dolly. I couldn't explain just now."

"Maggie, don't *talk* like that! You frighten me!"

"I can't help it, Miss Dolly. I'm worried."

"About Uncle Giles?" Miss Dolly crushed her cigarette against the top of the pale-grey suitcase, leaving a black mark on it. "He was all right when I left him."

"But you didn't see him leave then, Miss Dolly?"

"No. But—Maggie, I swear—I'd swear it on the Bible, if I had one here—I swear he was perfectly well and all right when I left him."

"I've got a Bible, Miss Dolly."

"Then bring it out, Maggie. I'll take an *oath* about Uncle Giles and then you won't worry any more."

Maggie did not move, did not stir. Nobody could do that, she thought. Nobody could swear on the Bible to a lie.

"But how did Mr. Camford think he was going to get away from here, Miss Dolly?" she said, after a moment. "When he couldn't telephone for a taxi?"

"I don't know. I didn't think about it. I was so upset, so miserable. If you could have heard the way he talked to me, Maggie . . . ! I dare say I'm not very prudent or thrifty. I'm not pompous. I don't *care* about the things Uncle Giles and Aunt Emily think are so important. But I've never done anything wrong in my life, Maggie."

That's certainly a lot to say, thought Maggie.

"I may have been thoughtless. I may have been foolish. But I've never done *anything* . . ." Miss Dolly paused. "Maggie, bring out the Bible."

Maggie took the little black Bible her father had given her out of her bag, and still kneeling on the floor, Miss Dolly laid her hand on it, her delicate narrow hand with the tinted nails.

"I swear I left Uncle Giles perfectly well and all right and ready to go off to Boston," she said, in a low, steady voice.

"And—Miss Dolly—you don't know where he did go, or what happened to him?"

"I swear on the Bible I don't know where he went after I left him."

"Or what happened to him?"

"Or what happened to him. But, Maggie, why do you think anything happened to him?"

"Because—" Maggie said slowly and reluctantly, "I found his wallet here in the house—all soaking wet."

Miss Dolly pitched forward on her face.

TWELVE

MAGGIE HAD seen other people faint; she knew what was done. She bathed Miss Dolly's face and wrists with cold water, and presently she opened her eyes.

"Maggie . . . I've got to *get away*—from this horrible house . . ."

"You must rest now, Miss Dolly. I'll help you get into bed when you feel better."

"I've got to get *away*, Maggie . . . Where did you find that wallet?"

"Well, that doesn't matter, Miss Dolly. Let's not talk about it any more."

Miss Dolly lay flat on the floor, her black hair damp about her white face, her thick curling lashes damp, her eyes wide.

"His wallet, Maggie . . . What was *in* it?"

"I don't know. Let's not talk any more about it, Miss Dolly. I'll help you into bed."

"I'm frightened, Maggie."

"Don't be, Miss Dolly. I'm right here."

Miss Dolly lay there looking up at the ceiling; faint musky perfume came from her, she seemed piteously fragile and helpless and stricken.

"Maggie . . . Mr. Angel . . ."

"Yes, Miss Dolly?"

"I don't know—how he died, Maggie."

"It was a stroke, Miss Dolly."

"Are they sure?"

"So I heard, Miss Dolly."

"That horrible Hofer man asked me so many questions about him. . . . If he ever finds out about the rowboat—what will he think, Maggie?"

"He seems like a sensible kind of man, Miss Dolly."

"I'm so frightened, Maggie."

"You must get to bed, right away, Miss Dolly, and try to get some sleep."

"Yes, I will, Maggie. You're so kind to me."

Maggie helped her off with the housecoat, and put her into bed; she was cold, her lips pale, she was shivering. Maggie went downstairs; she found everything in darkness there, she turned on the kitchen light, and boiled a kettle of water and filled an empty whiskey bottle with hot water.

"Oh, Maggie, that feels so good!"

"You must try to get some sleep now, Miss Dolly."

"Get me a drink, please, Maggie. There's a flask in my suitcase."

"Miss Dolly—couldn't you sleep without?"

"I *couldn't*, Maggie."

Miss Dolly poured out her own drink, and Maggie was no judge as to whether or not it was a big one. She tidied the room and she turned out the light.

"Leave the door open, will you Maggie? I feel—so nervous."

"Yes, Miss Dolly. Good night!"

"Good night, Maggie! I don't know what I should do without you."

Maggie got into bed and put out her own light, but for all her weariness, she was not sleepy. I don't know how it is, she thought, but now I'm *sure* something's happened to Mr. Camford. And Miss Dolly thinks so, too. Maybe she's got some good reason to think so. Maybe she knows something—or anyhow suspects something. Or somebody.

There were two people you had to think about when you thought of that wallet. Johnny and Neely. Neely was here in the house when we left, she said to herself. And when you think about how he acted about Mr. Angel . . . Mr. Angel was dead then, of course, but even at that how could he be so heartless about him . . . ? He's so queer and hard—about everything . . . And he was right *here*.

But Johnny went away from the duck farm in the rowboat. He was gone a long time, a very long time. It was sort of a queer thing for him to do. And don't really know about him. I don't know about any of these people. About Miss Plummer or the Gettys, or any of them. Not even Miss Dolly. When we were in New York, she seemed so different. She seemed to belong to the Camford family. But now . . . All this drinking and carrying on . . . Oh, if I could have a talk with Mrs. Crabtree, just for half an hour. . . .

A smug, self-righteous, common little thing . . . I didn't mean to be like that. I meant—to be a *good*, valuable person. I meant—to improve myself, and read, and learn things.

She buried her head in the pillow and cried herself to sleep.

"A few routine questions . . ." said Captain Hofer in a loud, serious voice.

There were footsteps on the porch, and a door closed. Maggie sat up in bed, filled with a sense of extreme urgency. Now it's begun, she thought. She got up and put on her dressing-gown and slippers, to go and wash in a hurry. But her door stuck; she tried the knob, she pulled and pushed it, and it would not come open.

I've got to get down to Captain Hofer, she thought. He'll have to ask me questions. The best thing is to get all dressed and then try the door again. If it won't open, I'll bang on it, she thought, and when she was dressed, she tried again. And she knocked at it; she rattled the knob and knocked louder.

Well, *that's* provoking, she thought. You'd think somebody'd hear me. She thought a minute and then went out on the balcony. It was a bright lovely day; a shaft of sun came into the tunnel and the water in its path was warm brown, flecked with foam. The rowboat floated easily, and the little launch; a fresh, steady breeze was blowing. I wonder . . . she thought. I wonder if I couldn't get in by some other window.

The floor of the balcony sagged under her feet, the railing was crumbling and broken away in one place. It's not *safe*, she thought, going cautiously close to the wall of the house. I'd hate to fall into that nasty dark water . . . . Here was another window, and facing it, sitting at a table, was Neely, drawing with a crayon.

She looked at him through the rusty screen. He's quite good-looking, in his way, she thought impersonally; then she scratched on the screen, and he glanced up with his clear pale eyes.

"Let me in, will you please?" she said. "My door is stuck. I can't get out."

"You can't come in here," said Neely. "Go back. I'll get it open presently."

"I just want to go through your room."

"You can't," said Neely.

"I'm in a hurry," said Maggie. "Just move your table and pull up the screen—"

"No," said Neely, and he began to draw again.

"Now, look here!" said Maggie. "I'm not going to stay shut up. I want to go downstairs *right now.*"

He did not answer, and she moved along to the next window, beside him. He jumped up and slammed it down and locked it. She went back to the first one.

"I'll smash that other window if you don't let me in," she said.

"Try it, and see what happens," said Neely.

"Whatever is the matter with you?" said Maggie. "What makes you so mean and spiteful?"

He looked up at her again.

"I understand women very well," he said. "I understand *you.* I know what you're up to. You think, because you're pretty, you can make a fool of me. Well, you're wasting your time."

"What are you talking about?" cried Maggie.

"Women mean nothing to me," said Neely. "When I was twenty, I was a fool. I'm glad of that. It won't happen again. Now you can stand there and make big eyes as long as you like."

"I'm not making big eyes!" she said, scornfully.

"You're a hypocrite," said Neely. "You deceive other people, but not me. You and your little aprons and your dish-washing . . . You—"

"Well . . ." said Captain Hofer's voice from below. "Very much obliged, Miss Camford."

"Let me in!" cried Maggie.

"Not I," said Neely.

A car started and drove away, and Captain Hofer was gone.

"All right!" said Maggie. "I think I see now. You wanted to keep me from telling about Mr. Angel in the rowboat."

"And you wanted to tell about it," said Neely. "You wanted to see me in jail. I know why."

"Well, why?"

"Because I didn't make love to you," said Neely. "I didn't pay any attention to you, and for that reason—"

She turned her back on him and went into her own room again. Someone will have to let me out pretty soon, she thought. I guess Neely locked me in. Well, Miss Dolly or Johnny will let me out. There's nothing to worry about. Only —it makes you sort of nervous, to be shut in. I never knew there were such hateful people as Neely and that Miss Plummer.

She made her bed and tidied the room. When I do get out, she thought, I'm going to call up Mrs. Crabtree again. I'm going to ask her to speak to Mrs. Mayfield, and tell her to find out if Mr. Camford really is in Boston.

And if he wasn't? Miss Dolly was frightened when she heard about his wallet. Maybe she'll do something herself. Maybe she's spoken to Captain Hofer already. Maybe I needn't worry so . . . She sat down on the bed, and she felt hungry. I wonder what time it is? It's not early; you can tell that by the sun. If only—

Somebody was trying the door-knob.

"Maggie, will you let me in, please?" called Miss Dolly.

"I can't get the door open, Miss Dolly."

Miss Dolly rattled the knob, and pulled and pushed.

"I'll get Johnny," she said.

And in a moment he came along the balcony and in through the long window; he dropped down into a wicker chair and lit a cigarette.

"Aren't you going to get the door open?" Maggie asked.

"I'll try," he said. "But I'd like to talk to you first. Getty'll be along any minute; there's not much time."

"I'm not going on that yacht," said Maggie.

"Dolly told me that," he said. "That's what I want to talk to you about, Maggie." He sat hunched forward in the chair, elbows on his knees, he looked strained and weary and bleak. "Do go, Maggie," he said. "It'll be only a week or ten days out of your life, and Dolly needs you."

"I'm sorry," Maggie said. "But I'm not going. I've got things of my own to look after."

"You're a kind kid," he said. "If I tell you Dolly's in a spot—"

"I'm sorry," Maggie said again, "but I just can't go on like this."

"Maggie, if Dolly goes off on Getty's yacht without you, it's the finish for her."

"Why don't you tell *her* that, Mr. Cassidy?"

"God . . ." he said. "If you knew how I've tried to talk to her. She won't believe me. Gabrielle Getty isn't going along, you know. If Dolly goes alone with Getty and Neely . . ."

"She ought to know better," said Maggie.

"Oh, yes," he said. "She ought to. Only she doesn't. She won't believe that Gabrielle hates her."

"Well, does she?"

"Why not?" he said. "Getty's infatuated with Dolly; he fell for her the moment he set eyes on her. *She* says it's just a beautiful friendship, and that Getty understands her, that he knows she 'isn't like that.' Maybe, I don't know. But it doesn't look that way to Gabrielle. She'll bring suit for divorce, and name Dolly, and that'll be the pay-off. You can figure out for yourself what that'll do for Dolly."

"She ought to know better," said Maggie.

He sat forward, his hands clasped between his knees.

"Dolly has a theory," he said. "She says that if she doesn't do anything 'wrong,' nothing can happen to her. It's a dangerous theory, and it's got her into plenty of trouble before this. But you've seen quite a lot of her. I dare say you've got a fairly good idea by this time of her romantic temperament. Well . . ." He sighed, staring down at the floor. "Well—I don't know any more to say. Maybe you're right, Maggie. Maybe you'd better look after yourself, and to hell with Dolly."

Smug and self-righteous? "I can't help it!" Maggie cried. "I *don't* want to be mixed up in things like this. I can't go on and *on*, trying to help Miss Dolly out of the mistakes she makes."

He rose.

"I can see how you feel," he said. "I'm sorry—I'm damn sorry, because I'm fond of Dolly. But I shouldn't have expected *you* to worry yourself about all this." He held out his hand. "Good-bye, Maggie!" he said, smiling down at her.

"But—are you going away?"

"Yes. I've got a job. I'm off to China."

She took his outstretched hand, and his fingers closed over hers; his eyes narrowed, as if in pain.

"You're a dear little kid," he said. "I wish . . . Well, it doesn't matter. Very likely nothing matters."

He was the only one here who had never said anything mean to her; he had been kind to her, nice to her.

"I don't mean to be—self-righteous about Miss Dolly," she said unsteadily.

"I don't know . . ." he said. "It must be a wonderful feeling."

"If I do go along with her—"

"I'd thank you to the end of my days," he said, and bending, he kissed her on the temple. "Don't mind," he said. "You wouldn't, if you knew . . ."

He went out through the long window on to the balcony, and Maggie stood looking after him with tears in her eyes. Maybe I will go . . . she thought.

THIRTEEN

There was a hammering outside the door, and a picking at the lock, and after a time, Miss Dolly came in through the window.

"They can't seem to get the door open," she said. "Something's happened to it. But it doesn't really matter. Will you get your things packed as quickly as you can, Maggie? The Gettys will be here any minute."

"Both of them?" asked Maggie.

"I don't know," said Miss Dolly.

"Miss Dolly, if I go with you, I've got to stop in the village, first."

"I can lend you anything you want, Maggie."

"I've got to get something in the drug store," said Maggie. "Some special medicine."

"Well, I'm sure we can arrange that," said Miss Dolly.

So Maggie began to pack her bag while Miss Dolly sat on the bed, smoking, scattering ashes on the floor. Maybe this isn't really so very queer, thought Maggie. I'll talk to Mrs. Crabtree from the drug store, and maybe Mr. Camford's home by this time. It's broad daylight, and people are coming and going. Captain Hofer came here. The door's stuck, but people can get in and out of the room.

Miss Dolly was foolish to think of going on that yacht without Mrs. Getty; she was foolish about everything, about coming to this nasty dirty house with two men living in it; she had been incredibly foolish to go to a money lender, and to sign papers. But being foolish isn't the worst thing in the world, Maggie thought. And if it's only for a week . . . A yacht . . . she thought. Me going off on a yacht . . . There was something faintly immoral about yachts, but undoubtedly adventurous. I do love ships and boats, she thought. And it certainly will be an experience.

"Let's go downstairs," said Miss Dolly.

"I'll make some coffee, Miss Dolly."

"If there's time," said Miss Dolly. "But we'll have to start the moment the launch comes for us. It's something to do with the tide."

They climbed in at the window of Neely's room that was empty now; they found him in the kitchen standing at the stove.

"What are you doing?" Dolly asked.

"I'm making coffee," he said. "I'm hungry."

He looked very neat and clean in a blue suit, his light hair brushed down, a little damp on his head; he began to whistle as he measured out coffee from a can into the battered tin pot.

"That's too much," said Maggie.

"We can use it all up," he said. "We're never coming back here."

"Never?" she said. "And where do you think you're going?"

"Hiram's late," said Miss Dolly. "He said ten o'clock, and it's after eleven."

Neely went on whistling, pouring boiling water through the grounds.

"*Don't* whistle, Neely!" said Miss Dolly.

He looked sidelong at her and kept on; she frowned and went out to the little porch off the kitchen.

"She's nervous as a cat," said Neely. "She wants to get away from here."

He seemed in very good spirits, and Maggie contemplated him with great displeasure. He let Miss Dolly pay his rent, and now I suppose he's willing for the Gettys to do things for him. Johnny's got his faults, but he isn't like that. He's got a job anyhow. He's gone off to China and I don't suppose I'll ever see him again. He didn't say anything about seeing me again . . .

Neely put his hands to his mouth and blew a bugle call piercingly loud.

"Oh, do stop!" cried Miss Dolly opening the screen door. "What can be keeping Hiram?"

Neely sat down and poured himself a cup of the strong brew he had made, and Maggie sat down opposite him.

"I hear a car coming!" cried Miss Dolly.

"Take it easy," said Neely stirring his coffee. But Miss Dolly had gone out into the hall, the front door opened and in a moment they heard her clear light voice.

"Why, Gabrielle . . . !"

"Hiram thought I'd better come," said Gabrielle. "Something very horrible has happened."

There was a complete silence, Maggie pushed back her chair and rose; when she went into the hall she saw the two women standing on the porch; Miss Dolly, so dark, so curved and supple in her yellow sweater, Gabrielle so thin and slight in a brown linen dress and a big yellow hat.

"What . . . ?" said Miss Dolly. "*What's* happened?"

"We found another body on our beach," said Gabrielle. Mss Dolly sat down on one of the benches.

"What—what *kind* of body?" she asked.

"It's like a nightmare," said Gabrielle. "It was another elderly man, very well-dressed, very dignified."

Yes, Maggie thought. You could imagine how he would look, lying there on his back, tall, spare, infinitely distinguished. He had made the same journey Mr. Angel had made.

There was a curious swirling inside her head, filmy thoughts trailing round and round. But they were coming to rest in a dim pattern. The awful thing that had stirred in her when she saw the wallet dripping wet, took form now. Mr. Camford was murdered, she said to herself.

"How horrible for you!" said Miss Dolly.

"Yes . . ." said Gabrielle. "Hiram sent for the police, and he thought I'd better come along and tell you—so that you wouldn't be waiting."

"Will it—will this delay our sailing?" Miss Dolly asked.

Gabrielle turned her head.

"We can't go *now*," she said. "They'll have to investigate this. Hiram and Captain Hofer will be here presently."

"Captain Hofer! Captain Hofer's coming here?"

"That's what he said," Gabrielle answered.

"Won't you come in?" said Miss Dolly with a sudden politeness and she held the screen door open for Gabrielle to enter. "Oh . . . !" she said, "that's Captain Hofer now, I guess."

But it was Miss Mitzi Plummer.

She came in smiling, wearing a dress of flowered chiffon, black, with huge red roses, over a red taffeta slip; she wore a red straw hat untrimmed, tilted at the back of her head, she had lipstick smeared around her mouth.

"Bon jour, la compagnie!" she cried. "Let's have a drink!"

"Something's happened, Miss Plummer," said Maggie, sternly.

"T-tut-tut!" said Miss Plummer, laughing.

"The police are coming, Miss Plummer," said Maggie. "You don't want to meet them and answer a lot of questions!"

"I *love* policemen!" said Miss Mitzi. "And why are they coming? A spy? I *know* it's a spy!"

"Don't you think you'd better start for home right away, Miss Plummer?" said Maggie.

For it seemed to her the last straw, the intolerable touch to this dreadful little scene, that a figure so grotesque should enter. There was no doubt that Miss Mitzi had been drinking; all these people drank in the very face of death. She wanted to get at least this one away; but it was too late, another car had stopped before the house, there was a knock at the door not like other knocks.

She opened the door, and it was Captain Hofer with Getty behind him. There was a policeman sitting at the wheel of Captain Hofer's little car, there was a battered old sedan that Miss Mitzi had come in, there was the big old-fashioned car that Neely drove, and there was a beautiful little tan roadster that must be Mrs. Getty's. It looked strange to see all these cars standing before the little house in the sun, with nothing else in sight in the flat, empty country, it looked somehow ominous, this gathering of people.

"Well," said Captain Hofer looking down at her. "Mrs. Getty here?"

"Come in, sir," she said.

He went in with a heavy tread, and she closed the door.

"Good afternoon!" he said to everyone.

"Oh . . . Sit down, Captain Hofer!" said Miss Dolly. "And you'll have a cocktail?"

"No, thank you," he said.

"Oh, do!" she entreated him.

And everything she said was wrong, and everything she did. She was much much too airy and sweet, he did not even answer.

"Mrs. Getty," he said, "this is certainly bad luck for you.

But of course, when the tide runs out, everything goes right along to the Point . . . We got your report at the station, but if you'll just run over it again . . ."

"I went down to the beach," she said. "We were coming here in the launch. And I saw a man lying partly in the water. I pulled him on the beach, and I saw that—he was dead. So I went back to the house and told my husband."

"Was there anybody else on the beach, Mrs. Getty?"

"No," she said. "I was alone."

"Anyone in sight. Any boats, for instance?"

"No. Nothing," she said.

"You didn't recognize the man?"

"No," she said, "I'd never seen him before."

There was something clear as crystal about her, about her words, her voice, her blue-grey eyes; the outline of her thin, fine body was so definite, and the way her fair hair was shaped to her head. She made everyone else look a little blurred, a little clumsy.

"Well . . ." said Captain Hofer. "No letters on him, no papers. Nothing to identify this time. I don't know if anyone here can help me?" He looked around. "Body of a man between sixty and sixty-five, height five foot eleven, weight about one hundred and fifty-five pounds. Bald. Wearing a grey suit."

Nobody said anything. Neely was leaning against the wall with his hands in his pockets, Miss Dolly was looking at Captain Hofer with her dark eyes wide. Maggie moistened her lips.

"That sounds like Mr. Camford to me," she said.

"Who's Mr. Camford?" he asked.

"But that's my uncle!" cried Miss Dolly. "And it couldn't *possibly* be!"

"I could identify Mr. Camford, sir," said Maggie. "I was right there in the house in New York with him for two months. If you'd like me to come with you—"

"We'll see," he said. "Miss Camford, when did you last see this uncle of yours?"

"Yesterday," she said. "He came here to see me yesterday morning."

"Yesterday morning?" said Captain Hofer. "And when did he leave?"

"I don't know. You see—we had a sort of—disagreement, and I went out. I went out and left him in the house . . ."

"What time was this?"

"I don't know. I didn't look. But I went out and left him—in the house."

"I met Miss Camford walking along the road at about eleven-thirty," said Getty. "She told me she'd left her uncle in the house. I persuaded her to get into my car, and go along to the Country Club for a bite of lunch. We got there by twelve, or earlier. It will be easy to check."

"Where was your uncle when you left him, Miss Camford?"

"He was—upstairs."

"Was your uncle expecting you to come back, Miss Camford?"

"I—no, I don't think so."

"What was he doing in the house then?"

"He—he was—he had some papers he was looking through."

"When you left, did you expect to return, Miss Camford?"

"Oh, yes! Oh, of course!"

"Did you expect to find your uncle here when you returned?"

"Oh, no! He said he was going to Boston."

"How did you think he'd leave, Miss Camford? On foot?"

"I'm afraid—I—I *didn't* think . . . I was—I was upset . . . I just went away."

"Where were you going?"

"I don't know . . . . was just—well—just walking . . ."

"Who else was in the house when you left?"

"Why, nobody," she said.

"Nobody," he repeated.

"Tut-tut!" said Miss Mitzi, suddenly, and he turned to look at her in severe surprise.

"What's that, Miss Mitzi?" he asked.

"Tut-tut!" she said with a giggle.

There was a silence.

"I'll just step upstairs and have a look around."

"This way, sir," said Maggie, and he followed her up the stairs to the floor above.

He stopped in the hall, looking around him.

"Was Mr. Camford drowned?" asked Maggie.

"I don't know anything about Mr. Camford—yet," he said. "The body hasn't been identified."

"Was the man you found on the beach drowned?"

He straightened up and turned to her.

"And why do you want to know that?" he asked.

"It's natural to want to know," said Maggie.

"You seem to be mighty sure it was Mr. Camford."

"Yes," she said. "You described him."

"Where were *you* yesterday morning?"

"I went out to lunch with Mr. Cassidy. We went in the boat to a farm."

"No farms around here."

"The woman's name was Mrs. Albee."

"Well, yes . . . They call it a duck farm. So you went there? What time?"

"I haven't any watch. I don't know."

"Mr. Camford here when you left?"

"Yes."

"Anybody else?"

"Yes, Miss Dolly Camford."

"Anybody else?"

You had to tell the truth and not think.

"Mr. Curtius."

"Mr. Curtius," he said. "Well, all right."

He started toward the French window.

"Captain Hofer," she said, "was Mr. Camford drowned?"

"I don't know if it is Mr. Camford."

"Was the man you found drowned?"

He made a wonderful face, his lips pursed, his forehead corrugated.

"You're in a hurry," he said. "These things take time, young lady. We have to have an autopsy before we can—"

"Oh!" she said.

"What's the matter?"

"It just seems sort of awful, when it's someone you know."

"By the way—" he said, "which is Cassidy's room?"

"Oh . . ." she said again. "Oh, that's it."

He went to the open window and looked in. "Yes . . ." he said. "Yes . . . Now, what about Cassidy? What's your impression of him?"

"Well . . . It's hard to say."

"Quarrelsome, isn't he? Heavy drinker?"

"Well . . . I don't think he's quarrelsome."

"Oh, you don't? Drinker?"

"He drinks—sometimes."

"What is his relation to Miss Camford?"

"I don't know."

She stood before him, her eyes lowered, her heart racing. Two years ago she had gone with a neighbour to visit her son in prison, and she would never forget what that was like, or how she had felt. She had seen men arrested too, one of them fighting and shouting until he was knocked out. She profoundly respected Justice; she adored order and propriety. But an unsuspected and passionate rebellion rose in her again being the instrument of justice. It was not in her nature to be the instrument of anything.

Her Covenanting ancestors had made many a bargain with the Lord, and she now proposed a bargain to Captain Hofer, representing temporal power.

"I'll answer any questions you ask me," she said. "I'll tell the truth."

"Very good!" he said. "If you have any information relative to these two deaths, let's have it."

"Ask me questions and I'll answer them," said Maggie.

"*That* won't do," he said. "It's your duty to volunteer any information you may have."

"It's my duty to tell the truth," said Maggie.

"Now, see here!" he said. "It's a mighty serious thing to withhold evidence."

"I've answered every question asked me, so far," said Maggie, "and I'll keep right on."

"This," he said, "is a matter of life and death, young lady. You can't make a game out of it."

There she stood with her eyes lowered, a high colour in her cheeks, her hands like ice.

"If you'll just ask me questions . . ." she said.

"Have you any information?"

There was a silence.

"You mean," he said, "that you've got information, and you're going to make me get it out of you word by word. All right. All right! I can do it."

She raised her eyes, and he was glowering.

"I treat everybody fairly and decently," he said. "I give everybody a break. *But—*" He paused. "If anybody gets tough with me, believe me, young lady, I can be plenty tough myself."

Pooh! thought Maggie. Captain Hofer failed to alarm her.

FOURTEEN

SHE FOLLOWED Captain Hofer down to the dining-room where all the others were assembled, and she was startled to see Johnny there, sitting on the edge of the table. If he knows about the wallet, she thought, maybe he'll tell Captain Hofer now. I just don't feel like telling him yet.

No, I don't think Johnny's a murderer. He does drink too much. He does talk in a sort of reckless, wild way. But it seems to me there are some good things about him . . .

"Miss Camford," said Captain Hofer, "I'm sorry, but I'll have to ask you to come with me—"

"Oh no!" she cried. "You can't . . . You can't—arrest me!"

"I'm not arresting you," he said, as if a little injured. "It's a question of identifying deceased—"

"I can't!" she said almost in a scream. "I *can't* go to that awful place again . . . I can't! I can't! I *can't do it!*"

"I'll go," said Maggie.

"We'd like to have a relative," he said. "It won't take you more—"

"I can't!" Miss Dolly cried. "I won't! I won't be dragged to that horrible place again. . . . I won't! I don't know anything about what happened. I won't—"

"Take it a little easy, Dolly," said Johnny. "If this man isn't your uncle, well, there's an end of it."

Hiram Getty spoke to her in a voice too low for anyone else to hear; he stood beside her chair with his hand on the back, a broad strong hand with a ridge of black hair. She listened to him, she raised her eyes to his face with a dazed look; she listened to him.

"All right!" she said to Hofer, "I'll go. But I think it's—barbarous, to make me."

"Then we'll get going," said Captain Hofer. "In the meantime I'd like the rest of you kindly to remain where you are until we come back."

"Now, people!" said Miss Mitzi. "Let's get together and solve this case before Captain Hofer comes back."

Maggie went up the stairs. She got Miss Dolly's hat and purse from the bedroom, and as she started down the stairs again, she heard an argument going on between Captain Hofer and Johnny.

"Be reasonable," said Johnny. "Look at the telegram for yourself. I can't afford to miss this."

"Everyone's got to stay here," said Hofer. "For the time being."

"I'll come back," Johnny said. "But this is a guy I've been trying to see for weeks."

"Nobody's going to leave the house yet," said Hofer.

"Captain, dear," said Johnny. "I didn't did it. I wasn't here. You know Mrs. Albee. A fine honest woman, descendant of generations of clam diggers. Ask her. She'll tell you what time Miss MacGowan and I got to the duck farm."

"What time you got to the duck farm doesn't interest me," said Captain Hofer.

"But it's an alibi," said Johnny.

"Is it?" said Hofer. "How d'you know what time to have an alibi for?"

"But I've got an alibi for *all* times."

"All right. We'll take that up later. I'll be back before long—"

"Captain, dear, take me with you then, and let me call up New York. You wouldn't like to feel that you'd ruined my future, would you?"

"A few hours isn't going to make any difference."

"Ah! Look at that telegram! Contact me immediately at St. Pol. Lentz. See? Says immediately."

"No."

"Just let me telephone. Just take me along, and I'll sit in the car like a little mouse."

"Well . . ." said Hofer, slowly. "All right! I'll do that."

He and Dolly and Johnny went out of the house, the policeman got out of the little car and came up on the porch and sat there.

"Now, people!" said Miss Mitzi. "Gather round! Let's solve this case! First, let's see about our alibis."

"No sense in this," said Getty. "We don't know who the dead man is."

"It's Dolly's uncle," said Miss Mitzi.

"We don't know that."

"*I* do," she said. "And if Dolly left him alive at eleven-thirty, all alone in the house—"

"I understood that he wasn't alone," said Getty.

"You think I was here?" said Neely.

"That's what I understood," said Getty.

They hated each other; you could see that in their faces.

"You're wrong," said Neely. "I was at Mitzi's, hours before that. I got to her house before eleven-thirty, and it's a good forty minutes' walk."

"That's true, Neely," said Miss Mitzi.

"Nobody knows when this man was killed," said Neely. "Only they found him on your beach."

"What do you mean by that?" said Getty.

"Me? I don't mean anything. I don't care anything about these dead men. Two men dead, well, what's that? Nothing. Only I'm not going to be bothered about them."

"No?"

"No," said Neely.

Gabrielle Getty rose and went out of the dining-room; Maggie saw her standing in the little hall, looking about her with a sort of despair, and she went out after her.

"Is there anything you want, Mrs. Getty?" she asked.

"I thought perhaps I could find some place to go," said Gabrielle. "Some place where it's quieter."

"There's the porch," said Maggie, and they went out there together.

"It's a—queer house, isn't it?" said Gabrielle.

"Yes, it's very queer," said Maggie.

Gabrielle stood at the edge of the steps, tall and slight.

"I don't understand these people," she said in her clear, even voice. "I don't know anything about artistic people." She paused for a moment. "I don't like them," she said.

"Well . . ." said Maggie. "I dare say that when you get to know them they're all right."

"I'd never like them," said Gabrielle. "I—I suppose I'm too conventional. I've been told so. I—" She paused again. "I think you understand," she said.

"Well, I guess I'm pretty conventional myself," Maggie said soberly.

She sat on the bench and Gabrielle stood motionless by the steps; they were both silent for a long time.

"I don't quite know what to do," said Gabrielle at last, and her clear voice was a little unsteady. "I got a letter this morning, an anonymous letter. I'd have destroyed it, I'd have—put it out of my mind, if it hadn't been for this—this new thing that's happened. But now . . ."

She opened her big square purse and took out an envelope; there was a letter in it typed on cheap white paper; she handed it to Maggie.

Mrs. Getty. You are going to lose your husband if you don't look out. The Bitch in the Boathouse is after him. She is a man-eater. One man is dead and *there are going to be others*. Look out.

A Friend.

Maggie read it twice.

"You'll show it to Captain Hofer, won't you, Mrs. Getty?" she asked.

"I don't want to," said Gabrielle. "It would only make trouble. I meant to show it to Miss Camford, but—I couldn't. I don't understand her. I'm sorry, but I don't like her. I think that perhaps if you showed her this letter, she'd go away."

"Well . . ." said Maggie. "I'll show it to her, Mrs. Getty . . ."

"I didn't want to take this cruise with her," said Gabrielle. "But I couldn't very well refuse. Hiram is so very generous and kind to anyone in trouble, and he thought it would help her . . . I'll have to go—unless she gives up the idea. If you show her this letter, perhaps she'll go away. That's all I ask, for her to go away from here."

"Yes, I see," said Maggie.

Either Johnny Cassidy had lied about the cruise, or Gabrielle was lying. She did not think it was Gabrielle.

Gabrielle sat down; she sat where Mr. Camford had sat. And he's dead, Maggie thought. He came here like Mr. Angel. He came for the same reason, to get Miss Dolly to go home. And now he's dead. If nobody else tells about that wallet, I'll have to. *I'll have to.*

Only you don't like to tell when you don't know what's happened. Maybe Mr. Camford had an accident, too, and telling about the wallet might only make trouble for someone who hadn't done anything—really wrong . . . I think Johnny told me a lie about Mrs. Getty. I don't think she's the kind to bring a divorce suit and make a dreadful scandal. I'm sorry he told me a lie. I'm sorry he drinks so much. I'm sorry—about—a lot of things . . .

But if somebody killed Mr. Camford, if this is murder . . . It was hot out here in the sun and the bench was narrow and hard. I wish I could take a walk, she thought, all by myself, and sort of think things out. Before I have to talk to Captain

Hofer again. If only, only he'd heard about the wallet from somebody else before I see him . . . I don't like to be the one to tell him. . . .

A car came along the road now, a taxicab. You couldn't tell who it might be, or what was going to happen next. A dreadful thing had begun, and dreadful consequences would follow inexorably. The cab stopped and Johnny got out and held out his hand to Miss Dolly; she tottered and leaned on his arm; as the cab drove away, she leaned against him.

"Take it easy!" he said, and led her along the path to the steps. "Come on!" he said, gently. "Come in and have a drink, and you'll feel better."

Maggie followed them into the dining-room.

"Well!" cried Miss Plummer. "It was your uncle, wasn't it?"

"No," said Miss Dolly. It was someone—I'd never seen. A stranger. But it was a horrible experience."

FIFTEEN

MISS PLUMMER had one of her unaccountable changes of mood; she became compassionate and almost affectionate toward Miss Dolly.

"Poor darling!" she said. "You must come home with me, and I'll cheer you up."

"We might all go somewhere," said Miss Dolly. "To Seaview Inn, perhaps—"

"Let's!" said Miss Plummer. "Music and bright lights. Let's go, good people!"

"I'm sorry," said Gabrielle distinctly, "but I'm going home. Are you coming with me, Hiram?"

He glanced at Dolly, and he might as well have spoken aloud to her, asking, shall I go with her, or stay with you. She lowered her eyes, and he turned to his wife.

"We can all start together," said Miss Plummer. "Neely, you're coming, of course? And Johnny?"

"Miss MacGowan," said Gabrielle, "won't you come home to dinner with me?"

That was the nicest thing, the kindest thing, the most courteous thing.

"Thank you," Maggie said, a little unsteadily, "but I—I've got things to do."

"Then will you have lunch with me to-morrow?"

"Thank you! Yes. Thank you."

"Then I'll send the car. At twelve?"

She held out her hand, and her thin fingers, cold as ice, closed on Maggie's. She's really a lady, Maggie thought. All the others are just—riff-raff. That's what they are.

"Come on, good people!" Miss Mitzi called out.

"Maggie," said Miss Dolly, very doubtfully, "would you like to come along?"

"No, I wouldn't!" said Maggie. "When will you be back, Miss Dolly?"

"Oh . . . Pretty soon, Maggie."

"Late?"

"Oh, no, I'll be early, Maggie."

They all began to move toward the door, and Maggie watched them. Riff-raff, all of them. No exceptions. Even Johnny Cassidy who had once seemed the best of the lot. I don't believe that story he told me about Mrs. Getty and the divorce suit, she thought. I believe it was just to make me go on that yacht. And why . . . ?

She sat down on the porch to think things over. It was very quiet here in the late afternoon sun, no sound but the insects chirping in the grass, the breeze was fresh against her face. I need this time, she said to herself. Because it's come now, the kind of crisis I felt was coming. I know it's Mr. Camford that they found on the beach.

Here's where he sat talking to me, and now he's dead. Neely tried to get Mr. Angel out of the way, just to dump him into the water and get him away from here. Now Miss Dolly's trying to do that to Mr. Camford. Just to get him out of the way.

Well, it *won't work*. Because I won't let it. Mr. Camford's going to have a decent funeral, in his own name. He's not going to be just shoved out of sight. I don't know how he died, but Captain Hofer will find out. And if it was murder . . .

I think it was murder, she said to herself, curiously calm about it. She got up after a while and went into the kitchen to get some supper for herself. But there was the kitchen in all the familiar disorder, the dirty glasses, the cigarette butts on the floor. She could not eat in such a place. She cleaned it up and put on the kettle, and now it was growing dark. She stood by the window waiting for the water to boil, and there was the rowboat floating on the darkening water. The rowboat Mr. Angel had been lying in, the rowboat Johnny had left the duck farm in for such a long time.

She was alone in this house without a telephone; there was no one anywhere who was concerned about her. Her mother would be thinking of her as safe and snug in the Camford house in New York. Mrs. Crabtree couldn't have any idea what sort of place she was in.

She turned on the kitchen light, and made tea, and ate some crackers. I'm going to bed now, she thought. There isn't anything I can do to-night. But to-morrow, somehow, I'm going to get to see Mr. Camford. And nobody can stop me.

She left a light in the hall, and she turned on the light in the upper hall. The door of her room was still shut, she had to go through Neely's and Johnny's room and out of their window, and along that balcony. I don't know, she said to herself, I feel sort of nervous. She went into Miss Dolly's little room, she looked in the closet and under the bed. Her own divan seemed a solid thing, but she got down on her knees, just to see. It was not solid; underneath it was a dark cavern where a lot of queer things lay.

She took down a shade on the roller, and poked out everything. There was an empty gin bottle, there was a book, there were empty cigarette packages, a pair of black socks, and there was a doughnut, green with mold, and gnawed. By rats?

She thought about water rats. Perhaps that was what she had heard flouncing in the water at night. Perhaps they could climb up and come in here, dripping wet . . . All right, I am frightened. Mr. Angel, and maybe Mr. Camford came here—up in this room . . . I am frightened.

She got up on the divan with the shade roller beside her, and she opened a book. Miss Dolly said she'd be back early, she thought. If I had a watch, I'd know when to expect her.

That bitch in the boathouse . . . One man is dead already, and there will be others.

Others. Did the person who had written the letter think that Miss Dolly had already killed a man? No! Maggie said to herself. That's silly. Miss Dolly isn't a murderess.

And how do you know that?

Because anyone would know a murderer.

104

Mr. Camford? Did he know his murderer at first sight? And all the people you read about in the newspapers? Do they know, so that they scream and try to run away?

They don't know. It is someone who comes up behind them—in the dark. Or it's someone who comes in the broad daylight; someone familiar. Someone who smiles, maybe, and speaks in a voice you know . . .

Have I spoken to the one who killed Mr. Camford? Have I seen—that one? I'm frightened, Maggie thought. I'm frightened . . .

It was not fear of any danger to herself that made her shiver, that made her heart race. It was terror at the thought of seeing a face and hearing a voice, and *knowing*. And worst of all, she thought that she did know already, in some unconscious way, and that one word, one gesture would bring the horrible hidden knowledge into the light.

I wish I had a watch, she thought. Then I could know—how much longer the night will be. Shall I go down and lock the front door? I mean, would I rather let them get in by themselves when they come? Or would it be better to go down and open the door when they ring? Miss Dolly and Johnny Cassidy and Neely . . . Which would come home first? And whom did she want to see first?

None of them. It was better, a thousand times better to be here alone, even with the water lapping against the walls, even with those things that jumped and splashed.

Someone was coming up the steps of the porch. Just one person, alone. Oh no! she said to herself, and cowered against the wall—if this is the one . . .

Then she had a vision of herself cowering and trembling, and it made her furious. She jumped up and went along the balcony and into the bedroom. The door downstairs was opening.

"Who's that?" she called, louder than she had meant.

"Me," answered Neely. "Is Dolly home?"

"No," Maggie answered.

He closed the door and began to mount the stairs slowly as if he were weary. Half way up he raised his eyes, pale and clear, to her face.

"You're *lovely*," he said, as if surprised. "You look like a nymph of the forest. You are very delicately made, and your hair is quite marvellous. You're much younger and prettier than *she* is. Why does anybody look at *her?*"

I suppose he's drunk, Maggie thought. They're all drunk,

all the time. But he did not look drunk; only very tired. He came up the stairs and into the bedroom.

"Don't go," he said, as Maggie put her knee on the window sill.

"I've got to," she said.

"I've got to talk," said Neely, simply.

"Then I'll come downstairs," said Maggie.

She was perfectly aware that he was unmanageable. Not violent, but blind and deaf to anyone else's wishes. He turned and went down the stairs docilely enough, he sat down in a straight-backed chair in the dining-room.

"You know," he said, "she's a fool."

Let him go on and talk.

"She's a fool," he said. "What does she want with Getty? She couldn't live his kind of life. She's a tramp you know. She couldn't live that life comme il faut. You can see *her* giving a nice little dinner party? Oh yes! Oh my dear Madame Dulac! So glad to see you . . . ! Then, if Monsieur Dulac is at all good-looking . . . !"

He began to speak in a foreign language, but his pantomime was deadly true. He was Miss Dolly looking up into a man's face with one of her long, earnest looks, her lips parted.

"Don't!" said Maggie.

He snapped his fingers.

"Okay!" he said. "But she's a fool. You must talk to her. You must tell her that she has to marry me. She promised to marry me, and now she has to do it."

"It's not my business to talk to her," said Maggie.

"You're her friend," he said. "Or she thinks you are. She told me you were devoted to her. I don't believe that, though. No woman is ever really a friend to another woman."

"You've got some queer ideas," said Maggie.

"In the beginning," he said, "she was quite wonderful. Somebody brought her to the studio I had in New York to see my work and she was quite wonderful. She had respect for my work. I was having a lot of trouble then, bills, debts, and all that, and she helped me. I couldn't tell if she was in love with me or not. She'd come to the studio alone, you know, and she'd stay late. But if I tried to make love to her—nothing doing. She'd be sad about it—*you* know. Disappointed."

Maggie said nothing.

"Well, I got tired of that. She's not a young girl. She's a mature woman. She's independent, she has money. She can do as she pleases. I said, if you don't love me, don't come here any more. Then was when she said, let's get married."

He leaned his silvery-fair head against the back of the chair and stretched out his legs; in grey flannel trousers and tan shirt, he had the look of a day-labourer, strong, compact, wholly self-sufficient. Love? Maggie thought. He couldn't be in love with anyone.

He was without the slightest consideration for anyone else; he was ruthless, bleakly aloof. Yet she felt the strangest compassion for him. Does he think Miss Dolly's going to get a divorce? she wondered. Or doesn't he know about her husband?

"I'd like to get married," he went on, gazing up at the ceiling. "I'd like to have a home. I'd work better without all this moving around all the time, all this worry about money. She can buy this house. I like it, and you can cook and keep it clean."

"Suppose I don't want to?"

"Then she can find someone else," he said. "That big room upstairs, that's the room I want. She can have a skylight put in it. Only I don't want to wait. What *is* she waiting for, anyhow? Do you know?"

"I don't know anything about it," said Maggie.

"We can get a license in two or three days. I want to get married now. I want to get settled. I don't know why she keeps putting me off. If I thought it was Getty . . ."

He shot out his arm and looked at the watch on his wrist.

"She told me she'd be home before this," he said. "I don't believe she is with the Plummers."

"But didn't you go with them?"

"I? No. I went to a diner and got something to eat, and then I walked back here."

"What time is it, please?" Maggie asked.

"Why d'you want to know?"

"I've been wanting to know the time all along. I haven't any watch."

"It's five to ten," he said, still looking at his watch. "If she's gone with Getty, there'll be hell to pay."

He spoke absently, almost carelessly; what he said was scarcely a threat, it was a statement. And the lack of violence made it shocking.

He lowered his arm. "You know," he said, "she told me Getty was going to do things for me. She said he was in-

107

terested in art. But now that I've seen him, I don't believe that. Do you?"

"I don't know anything about it," Maggie said.

"Is she in love with me?"

"I don't *know*," Maggie said in a sort of despair. "It's no use talking to me about all this."

"I haven't anyone else to talk to," he said. "Cassidy's no good."

"I think I'll go out and take a stroll," said Maggie. "I want some fresh air before I go to bed."

"I want to talk to you."

"Well, later on," said Maggie. "I'm tired, and I feel sort of nervous. I'll take a walk and think things over, and then I'll come back."

"Don't be long," he said.

"I won't," she answered. "Have you got a flashlight?"

"Look in the top drawer of that thing," he said.

She opened the drawer of the sideboard and found an electric torch. She made herself go at a leisurely pace into the kitchen, and out of the side door. But then she began to run, along by the wooden wall of the tunnel. Because she had heard the sound of a motor-boat, and she thought, what if it was Miss Dolly and Getty . . . ?

SIXTEEN

HELL TO PAY . . . she kept saying to herself in a queer anger. She stopped where the wooden wall ended and the water ran past the low bank. It was not a dark night, it was grey, with a faint mist from the marshes, like smoke; there was a rank swamp smell in the still air.

And the sound of the engine was growing louder and louder, a dreadful sound, inexorable, a machine rushing toward her. Hell to pay . . . what does she *mean* by saying she'll marry Neely, when she's got a husband? And if she cares that much for Neely, what does she mean by leading Mr. Getty on? A married man . . . No wonder somebody wrote an anonymous letter to Mrs. Getty.

She's killed one man . . . But out under the open sky, the phrase had a different meaning. It doesn't mean murder, Maggie thought. It means destroying men's souls, and dragging them down. Like the woman I saw in the movie, the one who ruined the bull-fighter. Miss Dolly wouldn't kill anyone. She couldn't. But she's a liar. She's—a bitch.

That was the first time Maggie had used that word, even in her thoughts. But it was just the word she wanted. She stood, looking along the creek that was like a dark gleaming ribbon through the misty land; the noise of the engine was loud and dreadful but it seemed to come no nearer; there was nothing to be seen. I don't see how Neely can help hearing it, she thought. Maybe he'll come out to see . . . All right! If there's hell to pay, it's her own fault. She brought it—

Oh . . . ! she said half aloud. For now she remembered Mrs. Amber. They bring it on themselves, Mrs. Crabtree had said. They get mixed up one way or another, with men. Like this. A tangle of lies and evasions, a net of jealousy and suspicion and bitter anger, until someone broke free from it, with violence.

Off in the march a green light showed, clear as an emerald; the boat was coming. The starboard light, she said to herself. Father taught me that when I was almost a baby. I've never seen another man like him. He was so—true . . . She turned on the torch and swung it over her head in a half-circle.

If only they'll stop, she thought. Stop here and not go on into the boathouse. There's Neely sitting in there, thinking about her . . . She promised him to come back early—but a promise doesn't mean anything to her. She's a bitch.

She swung the torch again.

"Ahoy there!" called Getty's voice.

Maggie did not answer; she did not want Neely to hear her. The engine was turned off, the boat came gliding along in a gentle swell that washed up on the bank where she stood; the light of a torch shone on her.

"Oh, it's *you*, Maggie," said Miss Dolly.

"And me," said Neely's voice beside her.

There was a silence.

"I was getting worried about you," Neely said.

"I couldn't get away from Mitzi," said Dolly. "You know how she is. And I didn't like the idea of her driving me home."

"Oh well!" said Neely with a curious heartiness, "here you are safe and sound. Are you coming in for a drink, Getty?"

"Thanks," said Getty, "but I'll have to be going along."

Neely held out both hands to Dolly and helped her out of the boat. The engine started.

"Good night!" said Getty, and the boat shot forward up the creek.

"And where's *he* going up there?" Neely said as if to himself.

There was no answer; they moved toward the house in silence. Neely pulled open the door and they entered.

"Well?" he said. "Shall we have a little talk, Dorothea, gift of God?"

"If you want," she said.

She looked beautiful and sorrowful and exhausted; her olive-skinned face was pale, her eyes were heavy; she raised her hand with that familiar gesture, and pushed her dark hair back from her forehead; her lovely narrow hand with scarlet nails. "I'll be down in a moment," she said and went up the stairs.

Neely leaned against the wall with his hands in his pockets; he looked, Maggie thought, more than ever like a workman, with the cool independence of a skilled artisan. She did not know what to do, she had no wish to stay here with Neely, but neither did she want to be with Miss Dolly just now. She went, with unhappy hesitation, into the kitchen.

Hell to pay . . . But she doesn't care. I suppose she can explain and make everything right. But suppose she can't? If Neely ever finds out that she's got a husband . . .

"Go up and tell her to hurry," said Neely from the doorway.

"You can call her," said Maggie, but it was a half-hearted rebellion. There was something about him that could not be denied, something savage, and something strangely touching. She got up and went toward the stairs. It's a mistake for her to keep him waiting, she thought. It'll make things worse. She can't play with *him*.

She was startled to see Dolly standing motionless at the end of the hall upstairs, by the window.

"Miss Dolly . . ." she said.

"Hush!" Miss Dolly said. "What do you want, Maggie?"

"Mr. Curtius says, will you please come down—"

"I'm coming" Miss Dolly said. "I'll just—is that a car coming, Maggie?"

"I don't hear anything."

"Get my red housecoat, will you, Maggie?" she said, standing near the door. And she was listening, you could tell that. Listening for what? What was it she expected? Maggie got the dark-red housecoat from the little room, and, standing in the hall, Dolly took off her skirt and yellow sweater. In her ivory satin slip with a yoke of écru lace she looked elegant as a princess, with her bare arms and shoulders, her full bosom, her small waist.

"Here's your housecoat, Miss Dolly," Maggie said. But Dolly did not answer or stir; she was listening. "Miss Dolly!" said Maggie, sharply, and she came to with a little start.

"Oh Maggie . . ." she said. "Neely's so unreasonable, and so unkind."

"Unkind?" said Maggie.

"I've tried to help him every way I know. But it's not enough for him. Nothing you can do is ever enough for a man. What a man calls 'love' is a *horrible* thing."

Maggie was not touched.

"Hadn't you better put on your housecoat and go downstairs, Miss Dolly?" she said. "Mr. Curtius—"

"I *dread* trying to talk to him. He's—sometimes I'm afraid of him, Maggie."

I don't blame you, thought Maggie.

"If I could only—" Dolly began and stopped. "Maggie! Isn't that a car coming?"

"Yes, it is," said Maggie.

"Will you go down, Maggie, and let—and open the door?"

She knows who it is, thought Maggie. It's someone she expected. Who could it be? I'd like it to be Johnny Cassidy. I wish it would be.

"Hurry up, Maggie!"

She went downstairs slowly, there was no reason to hurry; no one had knocked or rung the bell. Maybe the car had come this way by mistake and had turned back again. She hoped it was like that; an unreasonable dread had seized her at the thought of Miss Dolly's expected visitor. I'll just see . . . she thought, and had her hand on the doorknob, when Neely spoke.

"Don't open the door," he said.

"I thought I heard a car . . ."

"All right. Don't open the door."

"But it might be—Mr. Cassidy."

"I don't want anyone in here just now," he said. "Not until I've had my talk with Dolly. Get away from that door, will you?"

She looked back over her shoulder at him, and maybe he was worse than that unknown person outside.

"Get away from there!" he said and came along the hall toward her. She stepped back, and then someone knocked. Someone who must have been outside there for a long moment, very quiet. Neely beckoned to her by jerking back his head. But she was afraid to go to him.

There were three of them in the house, and somebody outside, and it was absolutely quiet . . . Everybody was waiting. And then there was another knock.

"Open the door. It's the police."

"All right. Go ahead!" said Neely to Maggie.

It was Captain Hofer and he looked different. He came in and closed the door after him.

"Mr. Curtius," he said, "I'd like a few words with you."

"Here I am," said Neely.

They went into the dining-room. "Sit down," said Hofer, but Neely shook his head. "I've received information regarding you," said Hofer, "and I want an explanation. Now then, Mr. Curtius, when did you last see Mr. Angel?"

"I don't know," said Neely, "I didn't look at the time."

"When did you last see him?"

Neely was silent, with one hand resting on the table, and the overhead light shining on his fair head.

"What's this about?"

"I'm asking the questions here," said Hofer.

"I'm not answering them," said Neely, "until I know what it's about. This isn't a game. If you've got anything against me, you can tell me, and then we'll see."

"All right," said Captain Hofer after a moment. "I've received information that you attempted to dispose of Mr. Angel's body by overturning the boat in which the body was concealed."

"Yes," said Neely.

"How d'you mean, yes?"

"I mean, I did that," said Neely impatiently.

"Are you willing to make a statement to that effect?"

"I've just made a statement."

"A statement under oath—"

"Oaths . . ." said Neely. "What damn nonsense the whole thing is."

"You think it's nonsense, do you?"

"That's what I think. Here's another statement for your collection. I didn't kill that man. I found him dead in the boat. I thought it would make a lot of fuss and bother if he was found here, and I tried to get rid of him."

"Did anyone assist you?"

"I suppose she told you," Neely said. "I got that girl there to row the boat. But she didn't know anything about Angel. She didn't like it when she found out."

Hofer glanced at Maggie, who stood in the hall near the doorway perfectly still. Neely smiled.

"I don't blame her for telling you," he said. "She's got a lot of fine old-fashioned sentiment about dead bodies. She's a *good* little wench."

He looked at her still smiling a little; the light shone on his thick fair lashes and gave him the look of a cat or a panther.

"Now what?" he said.

"Now you come along with me," said Hofer.

"Arrested?"

"Nope," said Hofer. "For questioning."

"God!" said Neely. "That's a bad word in Europe. All right. I'm ready."

"You'll remain here," said Hofer to Maggie.

They went out of the house and the door closed behind them. It was all very quiet and simple; just Neely walking off, hatless.

But it was horrible. He had been betrayed. He thinks I'm the one who told Captain Hofer, Maggie said to herself. But *she* did it. She wanted to get rid of him; and she's done it.

SEVENTEEN

WHEN SHE went upstairs, Maggie was startled to find the door of her own room open. Miss Dolly was standing in there lighting a cigarette.

"How did you get in?" Maggie asked.

"I found the key in Neely's room."

Maggie went into the room slowly.

"Miss Dolly—"

"I'm too tired to talk, Maggie, too miserable."

"Miss Dolly, we've got to talk. Miss Dolly, from the way Mrs. Getty described that man they found—"

"Oh, don't!"

"Miss Dolly I think that was Mr. Camford."

"*Don't!*"

"I'm going to ask Captain Hofer to let me see him. And if it is Mr. Camford, I'm going to tell the truth."

"Then wait, Maggie! Wait just *one* more day!"

"You mean it is Mr. Camford?"

"Yes," said Miss Dolly. "Yes, it is."

"Why didn't you say so?"

"He was—murdered," said Miss Dolly. Her mouth was oddly stretched and stiff, giving her face a piteous and almost ugly look. "They made me look at him—his head—" She put her hand to her temple. "Here . . . His *head* . . . !"

"Miss Dolly, don't scream like that," said Maggie, sharply.

"They made me look . . . First Mr. Angel—and then Uncle Giles—both lying there in that place . . ."

"Don't think about it, Miss Dolly."

"I can't help it! I can't help it! Oh God! I thought I was coming here—to be happy . . . Just for a little little while . . . But I never can be happy. I can't get free . . ."

"You needn't work yourself up so, Miss Dolly. Because we've got to talk about this, and get this straight. Mr. Camford can't lie there, in the morgue."

"Stop it! If you knew what that place is like—"

"Well, I do," said Maggie. "I went to a morgue once with a woman who lived on our street, to identify her brother. And that's one more reason why I can't stand the idea of Mr. Camford's lying there."

"Maggie, wait one more day before you do anything. One more day can't make any difference to Uncle Giles."

"But it makes all the difference in the world to the police, in finding the murderer."

"That's what I want," said Miss Dolly, faintly. "I want him to get away."

"Oh . . ." Maggie said.

It seemed to her that a sudden cool breeze came streaming in against the back of her neck; she looked quickly behind her. Nothing there, only the long window open on the balcony.

"Then you know—who it is, Miss Dolly?" she asked.

"*No!*" said Miss Dolly in a scream. "I *don't!* But I'm so afraid . . . If it's—who I think—then whatever happens to him will happen to me. I can't ever, ever get away from him . . . A woman told me that—a Frenchwoman . . . It's in my stars—"

"Miss Dolly, don't talk so wildly. If you know who it is, you've just got to tell the police. They won't let anything happen to you."

"Give him one more day! One more day!"

No, Maggie thought, I can't. I won't. But it's no use trying to talk to her in the state she's in. "You'd better get to bed, Miss Dolly," she said with a certain compassion.

"Then promise, Maggie. Promise to wait just one more day."

"I'll think it over carefully, Miss Dolly, and we'll talk about it in the morning."

"Maggie, lock the doors downstairs, and all the windows."

"I will, Miss Dolly."

"And Maggie, here's the key for your door. You can lock it now. And put a chair against it, so that we could hear . . ."

"All right, Miss Dolly."

She went downstairs to lock up everything, and she did it thoroughly, every door, every window. When she went up again, she found Miss Dolly closing the long window in the big room.

"Miss Dolly, we'd better have one of these open, to get a little air."

"No . . . No, let's close them, Maggie."

In a bad state, Miss Dolly was. She made Maggie stay in the bathroom while she washed, and she would not put her light out after she had got into bed. Maggie lay down on the divan and pulled the sheet over her, and got ready to think.

It's her husband, she thought. Her husband killed Mr. Camford. Or anyhow, that's what she thinks. Then he must have been out here . . . Has he been right in this house? She threw back the sheet because the room was so hot, so airless. It makes you restless, not to have fresh air . . . The bar of light shining from Miss Dolly's open door bothered her, too. Her arms began to itch, she got a cramp in one foot, the pillow felt prickly under her cheek.

I want to lie quiet and think, she told herself. I've got to think things out before I see Captain Hofer to-morrow. Because I'm certainly going to see him. And tell him. In a way, I'm sorry for Miss Dolly. It's going to be pretty bad for her when all this comes out.

Her discomfort was becoming frantic. It's just no use! she said to herself. I can't rest, I can't even think unless I have some air. She got out of bed very quietly, and looked into the small bedroom. Miss Dolly was lying relaxed and quiet with her eyes closed, and after watching her face a moment, Maggie crossed the big room and opened one of the french windows, opened it wide.

The blessed air came flooding in, damp and fresh; she could hear the lapping of the water, she stood there breathing deeply, filled with an unreasonable sense of relief.

"Maggie?" said Miss Dolly's voice, drowsy and gentle. Maggie ran nimbly back to her bed.

"Yes, Miss Dolly?"

"Maggie, do you know . . . ? Maggie, can he swim?"

"Who, Miss Dolly?"

There was a minute's pause.

"Neely," said Miss Dolly. "Can he swim?"

"I—don't know," Maggie answered, sitting motionless, waiting for more. What can she ever mean by *that*?

"Maggie?"

"Yes, Miss Dolly?"

"You're sure the windows are all closed, Maggie. The windows on the balcony?"

"I'll take another look," said Maggie, springing up.

She closed the French window and turned the handle. Could Neely swim? What difference could that make? Nobody's going to be swimming *now*, at this time of night, out there in the dark. Unless there were water rats. I wish this couch was solid, she thought, returning to it, with no room under it—for anything . . . I wish I knew the time.

But the morning will come, and then there'll be people about . . . I wonder if Johnny Cassidy's ever coming back . . . ? Neely will come back when they've finished asking him questions. Unless they keep him in jail. I'll be glad when the day comes and there are people around. . . .

But the person she found waiting in the dining-room was Mrs. Crabtree, composed and friendly as ever. How did you get here, Mrs. Crabtree? Maggie asked. Why, I came in the rowboat, Mrs. Crabtree answered. All the way from New York? Maggie asked, and Mrs. Crabtree smiled, and Maggie was afraid of her.

The rowboat was in the kitchen covered over with a tarpaulin, and she thought she could see something moving feebly underneath it. What's that in there, Mrs. Crabtree? she asked. Oh, just a duck, Mrs. Crabtree said. But whatever

it was, it made a sound, and she bent over. Tut-tut, it said.
Tut-tut . . .

She tried to rise, and could not stir, she tried to call
for Captain Hofer, and her voice strangled in her throat.
Help . . . ! she began to scream. They've killed another
one . . . Help . . . !

Mrs. Crabtree ran out on the porch, her footsteps making
such a clatter . . .

She opened her eyes, and it was day, and somone was
knocking at the door. She got up staggering with sleep and
hurried down the stairs, and there was another knock.

"Oh, hush up!" she said angrily. She opened the door,
and Captain Hofer and two other men stood there.

"Miss Camford?" said Captain Hofer.

"She's not up yet."

"Well, ask her to get up then," said Captain Hofer.

They all came into the house unbidden, and it was plain
they were taking charge.

"You tell Miss Camford that the District Attorney wants
to see her in his office. And come down again yourself."

Miss Dolly was sound asleep, and the sun streaming into
the room made it hot as an oven.

"Miss Dolly! Captain Hofer is here, Miss Dolly."

She did not answer; Maggie shook her and she did not
stir. There she lay, so pretty, so comfortable.

"Wake up!" Maggie cried and lifted her hand. Miss Dolly
opened her dark eyes.

"Captain Hofer is here. He wants to see you right away!"

"Oh," she said with a sigh. "Oh, Maggie . . . Will you get
me a cup of coffee, Maggie. It's—"

"They won't wait for that, Miss Dolly. You'll have to go
down right away."

"But Maggie, I took a sleeping pill . . . I was so nervous
and miserable. I can't just spring out of bed—"

"You don't want me to tell Captain Hofer *that*, do you?"
Maggie demanded.

"Then if you'll get me a towel wrung out in cold water,
Maggie, and a glass of water to drink . . ."

Maggie brought them and then she began to dress in haste.

"Maggie . . ." said Miss Dolly, still lying in bed, "don't
put on that black dress again. I've got an extra skirt and
blouse here—"

"No, thank you! I'd rather wear my own clothes."

"Maggie—it's *important*. You've *got* to look like my

117

secretary. Maggie, *please* don't be so stubborn about every little thing. It's bad enough as it is."

"Oh, *all* right!" said Maggie. "you'd better get up, Miss Dolly."

"In the closet, Maggie. That skirt—no! On the right. And the lavender blouse."

"That's too fancy."

"No, it isn't. Please don't be obstinate! And *please*, Maggie, try to act like my friend. Things are bad enough—"

The black skirt was a little too loose at the waist, a little too short. And the blouse of lavender chiffon with amethyst buttons and long full sleeves was far too delicate and expensive and fancy. But after all, what did it matter?

"Miss Dolly, you honestly ought to get up!"

"I am getting up, Maggie. But these sleeping pills leave me so tired . . ."

"I'll go down, Miss Dolly, and I'll tell him you're coming right away."

"Yes, and make me some coffee, please, Maggie."

Captain Hofer was standing at the foot of the stairs; very hot he looked, and angry.

"In there," he said. "In there," and pointed with his thumb toward the dining-room. "Now," he said, "the District Attorney's going to question you about this rowboat business. I suppose you know it's a serious thing for you."

"Well . . ." said Maggie.

"You know as well as anybody else that it was your duty to tell the police—a thing like that. You've got yourself in a very bad spot, young lady."

"I'm sorry," Maggie said.

But she was not alarmed. She could not feel that she had done anything criminal, and she did not believe that Captain Hofer was hostile. He was cross, that was all.

"And now," he said, "I want the letter Mrs. Getty gave you."

"Oh . . ." she said.

"That's just a little more evidence you were withholding from the police."

"I don't see how it could be evidence of anything. Just a spiteful anonymous letter."

"Oh you don't?" said he. "Well, let's have it."

She took it out of her purse with great reluctance; he glanced at it and put it into an envelope.

"I'm sorry," she said, politely.

118

"You're going to be still sorrier," said he. "Now, what's the matter with Miss Camford? Did you tell her I was waiting?"

"Yes, but she's not very quick," said Maggie. "Could I make some coffee?"

He gave her an outraged look.

"Do you realize," he said, "that the District Attorney is waiting to see you two?"

"Well, yes," said Maggie. "But it would only take a few minutes, and we could answer the questions *better* if we had some coffee."

He continued to look at her for a moment, and then he went into the hall.

"Miss Camford!" he called in a terrific voice.

"Oh, I'm coming!" cried Miss Dolly, and she came, wearing the yellow sweater again, looking pale, anxious and appealing. "I'll just swallow my coffee . . ." she said.

"There's no coffee," he said.

Tears came into her eyes.

"Come, madam!" said he. "We've got to get going."

To Maggie's surprise, there was a little crowd of people out there in the sun, and three cars. A man in a battered felt hat came up to her.

"Miss Camford," he said, "I represent the Evening Standard."

"No time now, boys," said Captain Hofer.

"You have any theory about this murder?" asked another man.

"Play fair now," said Captain Hofer. "You'll get your chance, boys."

He hurried Miss Dolly into the waiting sedan, Maggie got in after him, and he himself took the wheel. Looking back, Maggie saw the little crowd going up the steps of the porch and into the house.

"Are they allowed to go snooping into the house?" she demanded.

"Take it easy," said Captain Hofer. "I've got a couple of men in charge there."

He drove along the highway and into the pleasant tree-shaded village street; he stopped before a neat new building.

"Now!" he said. Miss Dolly gave a sob. She was still crying when Captain Hofer took her into an office, and Maggie was left in an anteroom.

There was a girl in spectacles who answered the telephone,

and typed very fast; there was a man with his hat on sitting in a corner and smoking. Nobody spoke. The typewriter clattered, the telephone rang, the man in the corner struck a match, and Maggie waited and waited. If only I had a watch, she thought. If I only knew the time . . .

She was strangely unable to think. Certainly she was not frightened, or even moved. The whole problem was out of her hands now, there were no decisions she could make, there was nothing for her to do. She was no longer independent, no longer free.

The typewriter clicked; what was the girl doing? Was she copying? Pages and pages about crime? The telephone rang and she answered it in a professional sort of voice, almost inaudible. Mr. Price is busy just now. The man in the corner lit another cigarette. I guess he's a detective, Maggie thought. A policeman in uniform came in, and went over to the girl in spectacles, he leaned both hands on her desk and they talked, very low. It was a long wait, very very long. It was so much quieter than you would expect.

And all this time it's going on, she thought. The law was moving in its course. Was Miss Dolly crying in there? It was a very long time . . . She thought of a movie that she had seen, a beautiful girl sitting in a chair, while the District Attorney stood in front of her, pointing his finger at her, shouting at her; the girl's luminous tear-filled eyes grew wider and wider in horror . . .

The door opened.

"Come in!" said Captain Hofer, and she rose and entered the inner office.

The District Attorney was a short dark man, with a long upper lip and dark hair combed up at the temples. He was a very quiet and serious man; he did not bark or snap or point his finger at her. But he disapproved of her.

He asked her question after question about the episode in the rowboat, and a young man sitting beside his desk took everything down in shorthand.

"I'd like to know the time, approximately, that Curtius asked you to go out in the boat with him," he said.

"I'm sorry," she said, "but, you see I haven't any watch."

He wanted to know—approximately—the time she had gone to the duck farm with Cassidy; the time—approximately—when she had left Mr. Camford in the house. He disapproved of her not knowing any times.

"You understand," he said, "that in withholding your information from the police you have made yourself liable to severe penalties?"

"Yes, sir," she said, "and there's another thing . . ."

"Go on."

"The day that Mr. Camford came—when I got back to the house, I found Mr. Camford's wallet there."

"What was your object in withholding this information?"

"Well, you see sir, I didn't know then that anything had happened to Mr. Camford."

"And when did you first learn that anything had happened to Mr. Camford?"

"Well, I thought when I heard Mrs. Getty describe the man she found . . . I called up his house to ask if he'd got home—"

He showed no serious interest in the wallet or her concern for Mr. Camford.

"This anonymous letter," he said, "where did you get it?" He knew that already. "Mrs. Getty gave it to me."

"Have you seen any threatening letters addressed to Miss Camford?"

"Yes," she said after a moment.

"Describe these letters," he said, and with reluctance she told him.

"Have you any knowledge as to the identity of the writer signing himself 'Othello?' "

"No, sir."

That was the truth. She did not *know*. And I do hate to be the one to tell about Miss Dolly's marriage. I will, if I have to, but I *hope* I won't.

"When did you last see Miss Camford's husband?"

"I never saw him, sir."

"When did Miss Camford tell you about her marriage?"

"After we arrived here, sir."

"You were surprised?"

"Yes, sir, I was."

"You asked Miss Camford questions about her marriage?"

"No, sir, I didn't."

"What's your exact position in that household?"

"Well, I'm Miss Camford's secretary."

"You're paid to act in that capacity?"

"Well, yes."

"Have you any knowledge of any letters or telephone calls from Mr. Haverhill?"

"Mr. who, sir?"

"Haverhill."

"I don't remember that name," she said frowning a little.

"That is the name of Miss Camford's husband," he said, and he leaned forward in his chair.

"I want you to answer carefully and fully," he said. "Have you at any time seen any evidence that might lead you to think the boathouse had been entered or used by someone unknown to you?"

"Why, no!" she said, startled.

"You haven't seen any articles lying about that might have been left there by a stranger? Think carefully."

"No, sir," she said.

"Have you heard anything that might lead you to believe someone was concealed in or near the boathouse? Any unaccountable noises, for instance?"

"No, sir," she said.

"Would it be possible for anyone to be concealed in the house without your knowledge?"

"Well . . . I don't know. Maybe it would be."

He went on for a long time about that, about doors and windows and where she slept, and what she could see when her door was open. It puzzled her. She had to admit that it was possible for someone to hide in the house, possible for someone to enter unnoticed by one of the three doors, or by a window. But she did not believe in it.

"Now," he said, "there's one more point. This Cassidy. What are the relations between Cassidy and Miss Camford?"

"Well, they seem to be friendly."

"Have you at any time heard Cassidy express hostility toward Miss Camford?"

"Why, no."

"Now, Miss MacGowan, I'm going to let you go," said he. "I'm going to accept your story of the disposal of Angel's body—temporarily. You did very wrong in withholding this information, and you rendered yourself liable to criminal prosecution. But you've given me a straightforward and credible account to-day, and I'm going to let you go. You'll remain in Miss Camford's house of course, and you'll hold yourself in readiness for further questioning at any time."

The look he gave her now was more like that of a District Attorney in the movies.

"Yes, sir," said Maggie.

"Have you anything more to say?" he asked.

"No, sir," she said. "Nothing that's—evidence."

He looked up at her with a nice little smile.

"You make a good witness," he said. "Just be straight-forward and co-operative with us, and you'll have nothing to worry about."

It seemed to her a very unsatisfactory interview.

EIGHTEEN

SHE WENT out of the office, not through the anteroom, but by a door that led direct into the corridor. There was a policeman there, and she spoke to him.

"Excuse me," she said, "but could you tell me how I'll find Miss Camford?"

"She's went," he answered. "The newspaper fellers was after her, and Mr. Getty, he took her somewheres in his car."

"Well . . ." said Maggie. "Can I get a bus back to the boathouse?"

"You could," he said judicially. "Only the buses don't run more'n once every forty-five minutes and there's a long walk after you get out. If I was you, sister, I'd get me a taxi and I'd charge it up to the expense account."

He liked her. He thought she was pretty. You could tell.

"Thank you," she said, and rang for the elevator.

"It's nice weather," said the policeman.

"Yes, it's lovely," said Maggie.

The elevator door opened. "So long!" said the policeman. "Good-bye!" said Maggie.

I've got to go back and stay with Miss Dolly now, whether I like it or not, she thought. But she's—the most selfish, thoughtless woman I ever heard of. She doesn't care how I get home. She'd go home and leave me on a desert island. She's like that to everyone. *Look* what she did to Neely . . . !

She went out of the building into the quiet, tree-shaded street. There were five or six cars parked along the curb; two women went by, one of them pushing a baby-carriage, the other carrying a string bag with feathery carrot tops coming over the edge; a little boy was coming down the steps of the library across the square. This was everyday life, and she was shut away from it, imprisoned in a world where nothing was ordinary and peaceful and seemly.

"Maggie!" called a clear voice.

It was Gabrielle Getty, in a roadster. She opened the door and beckoned to Maggie to get in beside her. "They told me you were here," she said, "so I waited. You said you'd have lunch with me, you know."

"That's *very* nice of you, Mrs. Getty."

"Gabrielle," she said. "We must be about the same age, I think. I'm twenty-three."

She drove the car through the village and out on to a boulevard that ran along the shore; here was the open water, sparkling in the sun; the salt air was wonderfully fresh and stirring.

"You know," said Gabrielle, "I told Captain Hofer about Dolly Camford's husband. I thought about it last night for a long time. I believe he wrote that anonymous letter. I think he's dangerous."

"Do you know him?" Maggie asked.

"No, but she told Hiram about him, and Hiram told me. Dolly wanted it kept a secret, but that seemed to be altogether a mistake. She said the man was violent and threatening when he'd been drinking. Does he seem like that to you?"

"I've never seen him. I never heard of him till we came out here."

"He must have followed her here," said Gabrielle. "She told Hiram she'd seen him in the village."

"Oh . . . !" Maggie said, startled. She reflected for a moment. "Well, do you think he's the one who—did away with Mr. Camford?"

"I don't know," said Gabrielle, in her clear, careful way. "I'm afraid I wasn't even thinking much about that. It was only that—" She was silent for a time, her steady grey eyes fixed on the long straight road ahead. "Hiram's very generous and impulsive," she said. "He's sorry for Dolly Camford and he might easily get into serious trouble, trying to help her." She paused again. "I'm not sorry for her," she said. "And I don't want to see Hiram in trouble—for her."

"No," said Maggie.

"I'm not sorry for her," Gabrielle said again.

The wind loosened her fair hair a little, and a strand light as a feather stirred against her temple; her face in profile was clear almost to sharpness. And it seemed to Maggie that

her nature was like that, too; nothing cloudy or vague in it.
She's unhappy, Maggie thought, but she can stand it.

The Gettys' place was breath-taking. This was an Estate.
They drove in through a stone gateway, and the house was
not even visible; they went along a road lined with noble
trees, they rounded a corner and there it stood, on a gentle
rise, a house of red brick with a white portico, neat, elegant,
impressive.

As they mounted the steps to the terrace, an elderly man-
servant opened the door.

"Any messages, Harolds?" Gabrielle asked.

"Mr. Getty will not be home to lunch, madam," he answered, gravely. "Mrs. Lawrence telephoned and a lady from
the China Relief, and they will both call again later. Are
cocktails to be served, madam?"

She glanced at Maggie. "No, thanks, Harolds," she said.
"We'll have lunch when it's ready."

She took Maggie up to her room, a cool and airy room
done in white and grey, with two turquoise lamps, a single
bed, no trace of Hiram Getty here. They went down to
lunch and it was served by the man-servant, assisted by a
young parlormaid who knew all the fine points of waiting on the table. Glazed sweetbreads, they had, with peas
and mushrooms, and salad and strawberries and cream. It's
a company lunch, Maggie thought. For me.

That pleased her and touched her so; everything she saw
here made her like Gabrielle more and admire her more.
She had those qualities Maggie valued most highly, she had
self-control and dignity and grace.

Conversation was a little difficult at first. But Maggie knew
her duty as a guest.

"I was reading a very good book before I came here,"
she said. "I'm sorry I didn't bring it along. *Anna Karenina*,
it was. I guess you've read it, haven't you?"

That turned out to be an excellent subject. Ever since
she had begun reading it, Maggie had wanted to discuss that
book with someone. She had tried telling Mrs. Crabtree
about it, but Mrs. Crabtree had said she did not care much
for foreigners, and that if a woman had a husband and a
child and a good home, and still couldn't behave herself,
she for one didn't want to read about her.

"There really are women like that," said Maggie. "My
father had a friend—another captain—and his wife was
like that. They lived on the same street as us in Brooklyn.

She lost her head over a Purser in the company and she ran away with him and left her husband and her two little girls. The Purser lose his job over that, and they lived in a miserable poor way for a year or two, and then she came back. And her husband let her stay. He forgave her. I suppose that's the right thing to do."

"I don't think it's a question of forgiving," said Gabrielle. "You can forgive anyone for doing you an injury, but you can't forgive anyone for—just not loving you enough."

All her life Maggie had longed for conversation like this, about books and ethical problems; her heart kindled, the color rose in her cheeks, words came to her that she had never used before, her thoughts took form; she savored the delight of creation.

"I've been to Russia," Gabrielle told her. "My father was sent there as a Naval Attaché when I was a little girl and we lived there nearly a year." He was plainly her idol. "I don't know where he is now," she said. Now she was alone. You could tell that.

They had coffee on the terrace and Gabrielle smoked a cigarette. I wouldn't mind learning to smoke, Maggie thought. Oh, this is like something in a dream! I'm so glad there really are people like this.

Harolds came round the corner of the house, dressed now in a chauffeur's uniform of grey gaberdine; he got into the car and drove off.

"He's gone to get us an evening paper," said Gabrielle. "We'll see if there's any news."

"Oh, what time is it, please?" asked Maggie.

It was half-past three.

"I'll have to go," said Maggie, conscience-stricken. "The District Attorney told me to stay there in the boathouse. And Miss Dolly won't know where I am."

"Harolds can drive you home, then, if you have to go," said Gabrielle. "But—isn't it a little horrible there?"

"Yes, it is," said Maggie.

There was a silence.

"Have you a theory about—what's happened?" asked Gabrielle. "Or would you rather not talk about it?"

"I don't mind talking about it," said Maggie, and looked out over the green lawn. "Only it's confusing . . ."

"I hope Dolly's husband did it," said Gabrielle.

"You hope—?"

"Well, you see," Gabrielle said, "he's someone I don't know, someone I've never seen."

"Yes," Maggie said, "that's better, of course."

So very much better if the murderer was someone you had never seen.

"It's logical, too," she said, with a sort of vehemence. "That husband's the logical one."

"If he wrote that anonymous letter—"

"I hadn't thought of that," said Maggie. "That makes it more logical."

"Dolly told Hiram her husband was insanely jealous. Well, he might not have known who Mr. Camford was and he might have been jealous of him."

It was difficult to imagine anyone feeling insanely jealous of Mr. Camford, but it was possible.

"Especially if he'd been drinking a lot," said Maggie. Why *shouldn't* it be Miss Dolly's husband? she asked herself, with that same vehemence. Miss Dolly thinks so, and she knows what he's like.

"Here's Harolds with the paper!" said Gabrielle.

She beckoned to Harolds, but he pretended not to see the gesture. He went round the corner of the house.

"He's so stubborn about bringing things on trays," said Gabrielle.

He wants to do things the right way, thought Maggie.

In a moment he came out of the front door with the newspaper on a salver which he proffered to Gabrielle.

She unfolded it and sat down on the arm of Maggie's chair. "Look!" she said.

Maggie looked.

POLICE SEEK CLUBMAN IN SLAYING

Police of New York City and Long Island are searching to-day for the clubman husband of socialite Dorothea Camford—

"But—!" said Maggie. "That can't be!"

"What can't?" asked Gabrielle.

Maggie did not answer; she went on reading.

Miss Dorothea Camford, an attractive brunette who gave her age as thirty, told reporters this morning of her marriage, some years ago in Paris, to Ewan Haverhill, wealthy clubman prominent in European café society. Because of the fact that Haverhill had recently been divorced by his first wife, Miss Camford decided to keep this marriage a secret from her aristocratic old Knickerbocker family.

"I intended, of course, to tell them later," Miss Camford said. "After they had met Mr. Haverhill. I thought it would be better to arrange it that way. But before I returned to the United States I realized that we were not suited to each other."

Jealousy, Miss Camford told reporters, was the cause of the marital shipwreck. "Even during our honeymoon," she said, "Mr. Haverhill showed an uncontrollable jealousy which had no foundation in fact."

"They make her talk like a servant girl, don't they?" said Gabrielle.

"Yes . . ." said Maggie.

Miss Camford stated that, although there was no legal separation, she and her husband had come to a definite understanding before she left him in Paris. "There was no question of any financial arrangement," she said. "I only wanted to live in peace."

Six months ago, Miss Camford said, she began getting letters and telephone messages from Ewan Haverhill, demanding to see her. She was at that time occupying an apartment in the exclusive lower Fifth Avenue section, but these messages so alarmed her that she returned to live with her aunt and uncle, Mrs. Calhoun Mayfield and the late Mr. Giles Camford. "No," she said, "I didn't tell them even then of my marriage. I didn't want to involve them in any sordid publicity."

In order to avoid the possibility of an encounter with Haverhill, Miss Camford rented a house in Sayresville, Long Island, and left New York without informing her aunt and uncle of her destination. "It was foolish," Miss Camford said, "but I suppose I was a little panic-stricken, and my chief thought was not to involve my family."

Miss Camford arrived in Sayresville accompanied by her secretary, Miss Margaret Gower, aged twenty-seven—

"Twenty-seven!" Maggie said aloud. But, after all, that did not matter.

"The morning after my arrival in Sayresville," Miss Camford said, "I saw Mr. Haverhill drive past the house, very slowly, in a car." Miss Camford told reporters that she had not mentioned her husband's appearance in Sayresville until she informed District Attorney Morgan Price this morning. Asked if she had any theory in respect to the slaying of her uncle Giles Camford, who had come to Sayresville to see her, Miss Camford became very much agitated. "I have no theory," she said. "I am entirely satisfied to leave everything in the hands of Captain Hofer. I have perfect confidence in his ability."

The police of New York and Sayresville are now seeking information in regard to Ewan Haverhill, described by Miss Camford as a man of forty-five, five feet eleven in height, and weighing approximately one hundred and seventy-five pounds with dark hair and a small dark moustache. When last seen by Miss Camford he was wearing a light-grey suit and a Panama hat.

Maggie looked from the newspaper with a blank gaze. But don't they realize . . . ? she thought.

"They're sure to get him soon, I should think," said Gabrielle.

"Well, I— If you don't mind, Mrs. Getty, I think I ought to go home now."

Gabrielle sent for Harolds and he stood by the door of the car.

"I've had a lovely time," said Maggie, gravely.

A feeling of complete unreality possessed her; she went down the steps of this princely house, to the car that waited for her, and she felt like a figure in a dream. But hasn't anyone else noticed . . . ? she thought.

For the description of Miss Dolly's husband was identical with the description of Mrs. Amber's Clubman, hat and all.

I don't believe there's any such person as Mr. Haverhill, she thought.

NINETEEN

As THEY TURNED into the road that led through the fields, a taxi was stopping in front of the boat house, and a woman got out of it.

"Why, that's Mrs. Mayfield!" Maggie said, aloud.

Harolds drove steadfastly on, making no comment. The taxi turned back, and passed them, in a little cloud of dust.

"Thank you," Maggie said to Harolds as he held open the door of the car.

He bent his head with dignity, and stood beside the car while she went up on the porch where Mrs. Mayfield still stood, ringing the doorbell.

"Maggie," she said, "there doesn't seem to be anyone at home."

"I don't think the door's locked, ma'am," said Maggie, and it was not. She opened it and they entered.

"What a peculiar little house!" said Mrs. Mayfield, looking about her at the dining-room.

"Yes, ma'am," said Maggie.

"This is—" Mrs. Mayfield's cultured voice was unsteady. "This is the most shocking tragedy, Maggie . . ."

She was in mourning, black dress and coat, black stockings, and an unexpectedly stylish hat, pulled too far over one eye. Her face had a bleak and ravaged look, and it occurred to Maggie for the first time that Giles Camford's death was a personal grief to his sister.

She remained standing, holding her purse in her black-gloved hands. "Miss Dolly, Maggie?" she asked.

"She's out, ma'am."

"The police, I suppose," said Mrs. Mayfield, and Maggie saw no necessity for telling her otherwise.

"I came alone," Mrs. Mayfield went on. "I didn't want anyone with me—until I'd seen Dolly . . . And on the train—I bought an evening paper—and I saw this other thing. . . . Maggie, did you know about this? This marriage?"

"Not till I came out here, ma'am."

130

"It was such a shock . . ." said Mrs. Mayfield. "And coming on top of the dreadful news—about my brother . . . I don't see how Dolly can endure this."

"Yes, ma'am," said Maggie.

"Ewan Haverhill . . ." said Mrs. Mayfield. "There's no doubt, I suppose, that he killed—my brother. And Dolly will have to see her husband tried—for the murder of her uncle. Oh, Maggie!"

"Yes, ma'am."

"I'm sorry for her," said Mrs. Mayfield. "I am indeed. It was wrong of her—very wrong—to tell us nothing at all. To come running out here . . . But what a frightful price she is paying now!"

"Can I get you a glass of water, ma'am?"

"No, thank you, Maggie. I've come to take Miss Dolly home—and the sooner we can go the better."

Like Mr. Angel. Like Mr. Camford. That was what they had come here to do.

"Mrs. Mayfield," said Maggie, "I'm sure the police wouldn't let Miss Dolly go away from here just yet. Mrs. Mayfield, I'll stay right here with her till she goes. Mrs. Mayfield, we can walk to the main road and you can take a bus—or maybe we might find a taxi."

"The police won't allow her to leave. Of course. I hadn't thought of that," said Mrs. Mayfield. "Then I suppose I'll have to stay here for a day or so."

"Oh, no, Mrs. Mayfield! You wouldn't like it here. It's—you wouldn't be comfortable. I'll look after things here if you'll go back to New York now."

"Maggie," said Mrs. Mayfield, with severity, "what is going on here?"

"Well, nothing, Mrs. Mayfield."

It's only that Mr. Angel came here to take Miss Dolly home. And Mr. Camford, too. And now you're here—and I *won't let you stay*.

"You have some reason for not wanting me to stay here," said Mrs. Mayfield. "You're not being candid with me, Maggie. I'm disappointed in you. I had such confidence in you, and so did Mrs. Crabtree. We both felt that you weren't to blame for this foolish and—disastrous running away in the middle of the night. I know that Miss Dolly can be very persuasive, when she's set her heart on anything. But I should think you'd have realized by this time what all this secrecy and deception— What's that?"

They both looked up at the ceiling. Somebody was walking overhead.

"I—I'm not quite sure, Mrs. Mayfield."

"Maggie, when I got here, I rang and rang, and nobody came. Was there somebody in the house all the time?"

"I—don't exactly know, Mrs. Mayfield."

"Maggie, who lives in this house?"

"Well . . ."

"Your common sense must tell you, child, that I'm certain to find out, sooner or later. You might just as well tell me now."

Maggie did not want poor Mrs. Mayfield to hear any more distressing facts just now.

"Well, there were some other people when we first got here, but—I think they've gone now."

Leisurely footsteps moved across a creaking board. The sun was shining into the dining-room through the grimy windows; the room was hot with it. The house was quiet now.

"Maggie, what's the matter with you? Are you frightened?"

Yes! Maggie thought. Yes, I am. Johnny's gone off to China, and Captain Hofer took Neely away and I don't know who's up there.

"I shall go up and see," said Mrs. Mayfield.

"Oh, it must be the plumber!" cried Maggie. "I'd forgotten. I'll just speak to him . . ."

She went running up the stairs. It was better to run and not to think. As she reached the top of the stairs Neely came to the doorway of his room.

"Oh, you?" he said.

She put her finger to her lips and came toward him.

"Let me in," she whispered and he moved aside to let her pass. She closed the door. "Miss Dolly's aunt is here," she said. "There's no use in upsetting her—"

Then she looked at Neely and her heart failed her. There was a dark bruise on his jaw bone and his mouth was cut; his pale eyes seemed blazing in his white face.

"What's happened to you, Neely?" she asked.

"I hit one of those policemen," he said. "And then they hit me."

She leaned against the door, overwhelmed by a feeling of helplessness, of utter inadequacy.

"What are you going to do now, Neely?" she asked.

"Now?" he said. "I'm packing up my things to get out of *her* house. But I'm coming back. Later."

"Neely—"

"She asked the police to lock me up. I know that. Because she was afraid of me. Before that, she talked and talked about getting married. I was to have a fine studio and meet all her rich friends and they would buy my work. I told her I didn't love her at all. Oh, what's love, Neely? she said. I don't think any more about love. My life's been so wasted, Neely, so sad and lonely. I only want to help you, Neely, for your good work. Fine."

"Neely—"

"Why do you keep on saying Neely, Neely? Are you afraid of me, too? The policemen, they thought I was a mad dog. Hey, you! Where's your papers? What are you doing, running around loose? They locked me in a cell. All right, I went to sleep. And as soon as I was asleep, they came in again. This time they brought a doctor—I think some psychiatrist, maybe. He put on a smooth, wise face. Ha! Now let's see . . ."

His curious power of mimicry evoked for her the image of a doctor, bland and superior.

"You don't consider human life very important, do you? he asked me. The war has changed your ideas, maybe? With so many people getting killed, one more doesn't seem to matter much, eh? And all the time what he really is talking about is a dead body—the dead Angel. Then he went on. In a time of such tension we find alcohol a relief, eh? Or perhaps a drug? That made me angry. I shouted at him and when the policeman told me to stop I yelled at him."

"Neely—"

"Neely, Neely, my dear sweet Neely, please be good. Go away now and don't bother me, Maggie. I want to leave before she comes back. I have something to do before I see *her* again. Go away. And you can tell her I said nothing at all about our fine marriage we were going to have. Maybe she meant to have two husbands together."

He took up a drawing from the table and put it carefully into a portfolio that he tied up with tape; he picked up a queer little black satchel. "Now I'm going," he said.

"Miss Dolly's aunt is downstairs," said Maggie. "She's—so nice . . . Please don't—please don't say anything to her."

"A nice aunt," he said. "A nice uncle, too, she had."

He looked at her and his bruised mouth widened in a smile. He put his hand on her shoulder and moved her aside;

he went past her down the stairs, and she followed him. Mrs. Mayfield was standing in the hall.

"Good-afternoon, madam," he said.

"Good-afternoon," said Mrs. Mayfield, politely, and he went on, and out of the front door.

"Maggie, who was that?"

"A workman, Mrs. Mayfield. He came to fix something."

"Maggie, he looked—"

"There's a car coming, Mrs. Mayfield. Maybe that's Miss Dolly."

They went out together on the little porch and Neely was walking off across the fields with the satchel in his hand and the portfolio under his arm, his hair shining like silver in the sun. Where was he going, so direct and unhurried?

It was Miss Plummer's car and Miss Dolly was sitting beside her. They both got out, and Mrs. Mayfield stood waiting in her long black coat, the stylish black hat over one eye giving her long face a sort of pathetic look, Maggie thought, like the pirate in that movie, with a black patch. She's nice. She's good.

"Oh, Aunt Emily!" Dolly cried and caught Mrs. Mayfield in her arms.

Mrs. Mayfield stood motionless, her head rising stiffly above her niece's shoulder.

"I thought you might like me to come," she said.

That was the best she could do. She would help Dolly, she would stand by her, but she could not make even a pretence of affection. Dolly, aware of the stony quiet, drew away.

"I *couldn't* call you up," she said. "I didn't know how to tell you, Aunt Emily."

"I see. . . . The police called me up, and I came. I thought you might want me."

"Aunt Emily, sit down, dear. And Maggie will make us some tea."

"And I'll go into the kitchen and talk to Maggie," said Miss Plummer.

"Aunt Emily, this is Mitzi Plummer. She's been very kind to me."

"Miss Plummer. . . ." said Mrs. Mayfield, bending her head. "Maggie, don't make the tea too strong, child."

Miss Plummer entered the kitchen in a gust of perfume. She was wearing a dress of dark-green linen with a great deal of eyelet work and she had a green silk scarf tied across her forehead, the fringed ends hanging down to her shoulders.

Obese, flaunting, gypsy-like; she was a dreadful woman, Maggie thought, remembering that scene in Miss Plummer's house.

But Miss Plummer seemed to have no memory of it; she was quite affable.

"Is there a little drop of something anywhere around?" she asked, in a low voice.

"I don't know what there is, Miss Plummer," said Maggie.

"All this upsets me," said Miss Plummer, looking around. "Have you seen Neely?"

"He's not here, Miss Plummer."

"They let him out this morning," she said. She opened the china closet and found a bottle. "I *need* a tiny swig," she said. "Morgan Price—what did you think of Morgan Price?"

"I thought he was all right," said Maggie.

"I knew him when," said Miss Plummer. "A pompous little monkey he was, and is. He tried to trap me about Neely's alibi, but I could see at once what he was driving at. The moment he said what *time* did Mr. Curtius come to your house that morning, I knew. I was plausible beyond words. I told Morgan the cuckoo clock was just striking eleven as Neely came up the steps."

She threw back her head and laughed.

"It was striking, too," she said. "But God knows what. It's crazy. It's a monstrosity we bought years ago in the Schwartzenwald, and one night when we had a party for some opera singers, we kept setting it at twelve and shooting darts at the wretched bird. It's never been the same since. But, my dear, what is time?"

Then you don't really know what time Neely came to your house? thought Maggie. Nobody here ever knows the time. And time is so terribly important in—all this. I know that. I've felt that right along. If I'd had a watch . . .

"Of course, now that this husband of Dolly's has materialized," Miss Plummer went on, "they won't bother poor Neely any more. Why anybody ever did think he had anything to do with killing all these people, God only knows. Except that the boy's an artist, and people like Willie Hofer and Morgan Price are naturally hostile to artists. He's a genius, that boy is."

The kettle was boiling; Maggie scalded the teapot and measured out the tea carefully. I don't know whether Neely's a genius or not, she thought. I wouldn't be able to tell. But I do know that he's—different. He's got a different point of view—and it's a pretty awful one. Heartless.

"Isn't this aunt of Dolly's piquant?" Miss Plummer went on. "I mean, the idea of Dolly's having these aunts and uncles and all this background of the utmost propriety when she's—what she is. The B. B., I call her. But I'm not going to tell you what that means!"

I know what that means, Maggie thought. The bitch in the boathouse. Miss Plummer wrote that letter. I'm sure of it. She found a loaf of bread in the bag Miss Dolly had brought with her; she made nice little bread and butter sandwiches, and set a tray.

"Will you have some tea, Miss Plummer?" she asked.

"No, I won't!" said Miss Plummer. "I'm going home."

"But—I thought you'd wait a little while and see if Mrs. Mayfield wanted to go to the station—"

"No! I don't feel one bit like taxi-ing Dolly's aunts and uncles all over the country. She made that poor besotted Hiram Getty drive her to my house after lunch and then she begged me to drive her home. Because it looks so much better to come here with poor old Mitzi, doesn't it? So *much* more respectable."

Her dark face flushed; she stared down at her empty glass and then flung it at the sink, and it smashed.

"*That's* how I feel!" she said. "And let me tell you this. If I chose to go on a diet . . . I'm not one day older than Dolly Camford, and I—"

"Excuse me," said Mrs. Mayfield from the doorway. "Miss Plummer, I'm sorry to ask such a favour. If I'd known there was no telephone, I'd have asked the taxi to wait. But, as it is, if you'd have the kindness to drive me to the nearest bus stop—"

Miss Plummer drew herself up haughtily. "No!" she said. Then, as she looked at Mrs. Mayfield, she raised her eyebrows and then frowned.

"I should be pleased," she said, with great dignity. "I'll drive you wherever you wish to go. I recognize a *lady* when I see one."

"Thank you," said Mrs. Mayfield.

She looked ill, Maggie thought, and she looked strange; her rather prominent brown eyes had a look of painful anxiety.

"If you don't mind," she said, "if it's quite convenient for you, I'd very much like to start as soon as possible."

"Certainly!" said Miss Plummer.

"And, Maggie," said Mrs. Mayfield, "I'd like you to come with me, please."

"Yes, Mrs. Mayfield. But—"

"I'd like to speak to Maggie for a moment, Aunt Emily," said Miss Dolly, standing behind her, and they went into the hall together. "Maggie," she said, very low, "please come back. As soon as you can get away from Aunt Emily without her knowing, come back."

"Well, why, please?" Maggie asked, curtly.

"I'll tell you later. I'll tell you *everything*, Maggie. After to-night everything will be all right, Maggie. We'll go away somewhere and forget all this dreadful time. We'll be happy—"

"I just don't care about being happy," said Maggie. "But there's one thing you'd better know, Miss Dolly. Neely says he's coming back, and he—well, he's dangerous."

"I can manage him, Maggie."

"Well, I don't think you can."

"I know I can. Only I've got to get Aunt Emily and that horrible Mitzi out of the house. You will come back, won't you, Maggie?"

"Miss Dolly," said Maggie, slowly, "I don't think I will."

Miss Dolly's eyes widened; she caught Maggie's wrist.

"But, Maggie, please! Maggie, I need you!"

"Waiting! Waiting, good people!" sang out Miss Plummer.

"I've got to go," said Maggie.

"Oh, Maggie, come back!" Miss Dolly implored her. "I don't know what I'll do without you, Maggie. *I need you.*"

"I'm sorry," said Maggie. "I've got to go now."

Miss Plummer was sitting in her little car when Mrs. Mayfield and Maggie came out of the house. "And now," she said, suddenly in great good humour, "now whither, prithee?"

"The nearest bus stop, if you please," said Mrs. Mayfield.

"Oh, no!" said Miss Plummer. "You want to go to the station, don't you?"

"Thank you, no. I have some little errands to do in the village."

"But I'll take you anywhere the bus could take you, and it's so much, much comfier. Just say where you want to go."

"The bus stop will do nicely, thank you."

"I just won't let you," said Miss Plummer. "Just won't let you take a nasty smelly ole bus when I've got my car."

"You're very kind, Miss Plummer," said Mrs. Mayfield, "but I'd really rather take the bus."

That ended the battle; Miss Plummer stopped her car on the highway and they sat in it until a bus appeared. Thank you very much, Miss Plummer, and you're very welcome, Mrs. Mayfield.

The bus was nearly empty; they sat down near the back where there was no one to hear them.

"Maggie," said Mrs. Mayfield, "I know I can trust you. Even Miss Dolly has nothing but praise for you. It's a terrible situation, Maggie. We shall have to stand by Miss Dolly. You see—" She paused a moment. "No matter what Ewan Haverhill may have done, he's still her husband."

"Yes, ma'am," said Maggie. If there ever was any such person, she thought.

"Miss Dolly is going to help him get away, Maggie."

"Yes, ma'am."

"It's a problem," Mrs. Mayfield went on, "a very dreadful problem. Whether or not she ought to shield him. I don't know, Maggie, what I should do in such a case. I don't know."

"No, ma'am," said Maggie.

It was difficult for her to say anything at all, so great was her resentment against Miss Dolly for this new and shameless deception. As if poor Mrs. Mayfield didn't have enough grief and trouble without that made-up husband getting into it.

"She wanted to get everyone out of the house, Maggie, because he's coming back. I can understand that she didn't want—she *couldn't* turn him over to the police. Her own husband . . . But, Maggie, I'm alarmed, I'm seriously alarmed at leaving her alone in the house with that man."

"Miss Dolly will know how to manage him, ma'am."

"I'm not at all sure of that, Maggie. She's not—very prudent, not very wise. And you read such horrible things in the newspapers. There's been a case, just recently . . ."

Mrs. Amber, thought Maggie. *She* wasn't very prudent or very wise. I dare say she was quite a lot like Miss Dolly.

"It's such an isolated house," said Mrs. Mayfield. "No telephone, no one near her. I was very much opposed to leaving her there alone—yet I understood how she felt."

"I guess Miss Dolly knows what she's doing, Mrs. Mayfield."

"I wish I were sure of that, Maggie," said Mrs. Mayfield.

They were silent for a time. The bus was spinning along the highway that was lined with woodland, the trees were quiet against the bright sky. They passed a little lake of shining water and as Maggie looked back for another glimpse of that charming scene she saw Miss Mitzi Plummer driving along behind the bus. Following us? she thought.

"Mrs. Mayfield," she said, "excuse me, but how long did Miss Dolly think it would take to—get Mr. Haverhill away?"

"She couldn't be sure," Mrs. Mayfield answered. "There's a great deal to be arranged between them, of course, and she thought he might need a few hours' sleep. But she said we might come back as early in the morning as we liked."

"All the way from New York. Mrs. Mayfield?"

"I'm not going home, Maggie. I'm going to stay here in Sayresville. There's an inn Dolly told me about and I shall stay there tonight. And you too, Maggie."

"Yes, ma'am."

"It may be very wrong of me," said Mrs. Mayfield. "But I do think that Giles himself . . ." Her lip trembled. "I do think that Giles himself would feel as I do. I can't help hoping with all my heart that Ewan Haverhill escapes. Not only for Dolly's sake—but when I think of his poor mother—"

"His mother, Mrs. Mayfield?"

"She's over eighty, Maggie, and she's a very conservative woman."

"But, Mrs. Mayfield . . . But, do you *know* her?"

"Not very well," Mrs. Mayfield answered. "We were on a committee together once, years ago, in the other war. I saw Ewan once or twice when he was a boy—"

"You *saw* him, Mrs. Mayfield?"

"My dear child," said Mrs. Mayfield, "why not?"

"I just didn't know you'd—seen Mr. Haverhill," said Maggie.

"I suppose," said Mrs. Mayfield, "that at your age the things you read in the newspapers don't seem quite real. But they are real, Maggie. Unfortunately."

"Yes, ma'am," said Maggie.

TWENTY

THEY GOT out of the bus in the square before the Post Office. There was an arcade here and in it was a stylish little shop, The Fifth Avenue Maison. Mrs. Mayfield bought two nightgowns and two pairs of stockings, two cotton kimonas, two pairs of slippers; what she bought for Maggie was just as good as what she got for herself.

"And a hat," she said. "You must have a hat, Maggie."

"I don't really need one, Mrs. Mayfield."

"You came away without any, the moment I asked you to, and it's only right that you should have a new one, Maggie."

She saw one that accorded with her taste. "Try this one on!" she said.

It was a triangular hat of rough and shiny black straw, with a rosette of green ribbon straight in the middle of the front, a hat that perched on top of Maggie's bright curly hair with a curious effect.

"Very nice!" said Mrs. Mayfield. "Don't you think so, Maggie?"

"Yes, ma'am," said Maggie.

She liked Mrs. Mayfield so much, she was so sorry for her that she would have agreed to worse than this. Five dollars, this hat was.

They went then to a drug store where Mrs. Mayfield bought soap and washcloths and toothbrushes and toothpaste, all the decent and ladylike things without which she could not envisage going to bed. They came out into the street and in a shop window Maggie had a glimpse of them, the tall gaunt Mrs. Mayfield all in black, and herself in Miss Dolly's elegant lavender chiffon blouse and her new hat, walking along this village street. The strangeness of life . . . ! They turned a corner and there Maggie caught sight of Miss Plummer in her little car, creeping along by the curb. Following them?

She hates Miss Dolly, Maggie thought. She wrote that horrible letter. I dare say plenty of other people hate Miss Dolly, too, and you can hardly blame them. But I don't want her to be murdered.

That was what was in her mind now.

On a corner opposite the tidy little railroad station stood a hotel, the Lord Sayres Arms; they went into a pleasant little lounge, and Mrs. Mayfield, with a paper package under her arm, approached the desk and engaged two connecting rooms and bath. She was an unknown woman here, with no luggage except that parcel, but that made no difference to her, or to anyone else; her Mrs. Mayfield quality was beyond question.

"And please send up a menu," she said. "We'll have our dinner upstairs."

She took trouble in ordering for Maggie, suggesting things she thought the girl would like.

"You're *very* kind to me, Mrs. Mayfield," Maggie said.

"You're a comfort to me, Maggie. I feel—" She paused. "I feel very lonely," she said, with simplicity.

She could not eat, poor woman.' She was half ill with grief and shock and anxiety.

"I cannot help worrying about Dolly," she said. "She's the last of the family left now. Her father was my older brother, you know."

It was still light when they finished their early dinner; they sat in Mrs. Mayfield's room, and she talked a little about her brothers, her young days. Maggie was touched; she would have been glad to listen as long as Mrs. Mayfield chose to talk, if it had not been for her desperate impatience to get on with her own thinking. The sky paled, the dusk came, and deepened; the lights of the station shone in at the window against the white wall; a little breeze blew in from the dusty street.

"You look tired, Maggie," said Mrs. Mayfield. "Go to bed and get a good night's sleep, my dear."

She had a book and a magazine that she had brought to read on the train, a Bostonian magazine and a book about World Conditions. She won't get much sleep, poor thing, Maggie thought. She'll be worrying and worrying about Miss Dolly. Well, it's something to worry about.

"Good-night, Maggie."

"Good-night, Mrs. Mayfield."

This was the first time Maggie had ever occupied a hotel room, and it impressed her. The bed was turned down and a lighted lamp stood on the table beside it; there was a nice little pink armchair, there was the bathroom, glittering with white tiles and nickel. She wandered about for a moment, looking at everything.

This is an experience, she thought. This is something new. My own telephone; someone to turn down my bed. This is a place you could really call your own, so neat and quiet. So—private. Nobody's going to come knocking at the door and asking you to do things. It must make people different, to live like this, in this peace and quiet. I've been so sort of busy, all my life.

A busy little girl, hurrying off to school, hurrying home

to help her mother, growing up busy, and proud of it. In nineteen years this, she thought, was the first time she had really felt alone.

And she would have to think things out alone, and act alone.

She sat down in the pink armchair. So Miss Dolly's husband *is* real, she thought. Mrs. Mayfield's seen him. But how can he look just exactly like Mrs. Amber's Clubman? I don't see . . .

Unless he's the same man.

That was a thought that made her catch her breath in a faint gasp. The same man . . . ? I'd better go right to Captain Hofer and tell him. . . . But I can't. Mrs. Mayfield trusted me not to tell. The same man . . . ? Mrs. Amber had been pretty and dark, lively, too. The colored maid had come in and found her lying dead on the floor, partially clad, Police Seek Wealthy Clubman.

He had a different name, but that didn't count. They bring it on themselves . . . Mrs. Amber and her gay parties. Miss Dolly and her relentless search for happiness. This man must have a way with him. Something about him that women liked and trusted. When he rang the bell, Mrs. Amber opened the door and let him in, and he murdered her. Maybe she had been waiting for him. As Miss Dolly was waiting now.

I need you, Maggie, she had said. But what can *I* do? If he came in with a gun . . . Why does she need me? If she's afraid of him, why does she wait there for him, all alone? It's —silly!

But she is silly. Maybe Mrs. Amber was like that, too. A little bit scared—but not scared enough. Only, Miss Dolly knows her husband's a murderer. But I suppose she thinks he wouldn't hurt *her*, no matter what he's done. Yet she can't be too sure. Come back, she said. I need you. After to-night, she said, everything's going to be all right. That's because she thinks she's going to get rid of her husband to-night.

She rose and went to the window, and stood looking out at the lights of the little station and down at the street, that was curiously alive in the dim-out. A moving throng of people went by; soldiers and sailors and girls; such a lot of couples.

I'm sort of sorry Johnny Cassidy's gone away, she thought. You could talk to him. I suppose you can know a man isn't much good and still—sort of like him. . . . A train went hurtling past the station, and whistled, that long-drawn, wild and melancholy sound that evokes all partings and lonely journeys. It made tears come into her eyes. I'm getting to understand more about human nature, she thought. Ah, well . . . !

She sighed, and her mind was made up, almost of its own accord. I'll go back to the boathouse, she thought.

But she was not going to take any foolish chances. She was not going to be stranded out there with Miss Dolly and a murderer. The thing was going to be thought out and done sensibly. She was ready to help Miss Dolly just once more, but she was not going to be foolhardy.

It would be nice to have a friend, an ally, someone to talk to; it would, she thought with unwonted humility, be nice to ask somebody's advice. It would not be Mrs. Mayfield she would have chosen for a counsellor. She admired and respected Mrs. Mayfield; in a way, she quite loved her. But Mrs. Mayfield was too much concerned with dread of family scandal, and she didn't, Maggie thought, know very much about life. Not nearly so much as Mrs. Crabtree and Johnny Cassidy.

But Mrs. Crabtree and Johnny Cassidy were out of reach and Mrs. Mayfield was right here. There was a small writing-desk in a corner and in the drawer she found envelopes and writing paper with a crest and a Latin motto.

Dear Mrs. Mayfield: I have gone back to the boat-house because I am rather worried about Miss Dolly. I hope to be back pretty soon but if I am not, I hope you will excuse me for going away without telling you, and I wanted you to know where I had gone.
Yours very truly,
Maggie MacGowan.

She addressed this to Mrs. Mayfield and then she put on that new hat. After this is all over, she thought, I'm going to have a different way of dressing. More stylish. I'm going to buy a lipstick and I'm going to be more up-to-date.

But when it was time to leave her room, new and disturbing worries came to her. She did not know how things were done in a hotel and the possibility of doing something conspicuous or laughable dismayed her. The best she could do was, to carry it off with a high hand, and when she went out to the elevator she had a look of cold disdain. She went down to the lobby and approached the desk, still with cold disdain.

"Good evening!" said the clerk, with a smile that she thought condescending.

"I wish to have a note delivered to Mrs. Mayfield in two hours," said Maggie.

"Certainly," said he, "if you'll give it to me."

"Well . . . you'd better make a note about the time and all," said Maggie.

"Oh, I won't forget," said he, and he was undoubtedly condescending.

"It's important," said Maggie.

"I see," he said.

He was a tall and willowy young man with wavy black hair, and she did not like him.

"If there's any charge—" she said.

"Charge?" he said, as if astonished. "Oh, no. No, indeed. Mrs.—" He glanced at a typed list lying near him. "Miss MacGowan," he said, "don't worry. We manage to deliver a good many important notes, Miss MacGowan. Mrs. Mayfield will get hers safely."

"Well . . ." said Maggie. She could think of nothing else to say, nothing to impress this young man. "Well, I hope she does," she said, with an almost sinister look at him.

She went out with the idea of crossing the street to the station, where she had seen a taxi waiting. But there was a taxi now in front of the hotel, with the driver reading a newspaper.

"Do you know where the boathouse is?" she asked.

"Miss Plummer's?" said he. "Yep. I know."

"I want to go there," said Maggie. "And I want you to wait—for quite a long while."

"Why not?" said he.

He was a stolid young man in his shirtsleeves, with a pale face and heavy-lidded eyes and a lock of black hair flattened against his forehead; he had a calmness that was reassuring to her. She got into the cab, and they set off along the village street.

"There is certainly some peculiar things happening out there," the driver observed. "I took out two other people for the papers this afternoon. What I think is, you people on the papers know more than the cops. I'll tell you why I think like that."

He told her a story, a long story about a murder, which he

said, had been solved by his favourite New York newspaper. "The cops was stuck," he said, "and I'll tell you why. The cops are okay—up to a certain point. They got organization, some of them have good brains. Some, not all. Where they fall down is, they don't dee-duce. Now, take for instance how these newspapers babies are talking right in my cab this afternoon. This first guy that died. The doctors say he didn't die easy. It took him twenty minutes, they say, before he died, according to what the doctors say. He got a crack on the back of the head when he fell in the rowboat, and he's lying in that boat there, bleeding, kind of feebly moving—"

"Don't!" said Maggie. "I don't like to hear about it."

"Well, but facts has got to be faced," said the driver, aggrieved. "And I'll tell you why. Now las' year this guy I know, a truck runs over him. The *way* he was marked—!"

"I don't *want* to hear about things like that!" cried Maggie.

"*All* right! *All* right!" said the driver. "If you don't want to face facts, all right, don't face them. I got an interest in this case, and I'll tell you why. I like to exercise my brains. You got to exercise your brains just like you exercise your body. I figured out how it could be with this other baby, the one that's her uncle."

It was shocking to hear Mr. Camford spoken of like that. "He was a very fine man," said Maggie.

"Maybe," said the driver, "and maybe not. The interest I got in this case is, who is guilty. Now, from what I read in the papers, they all of them got alibis for the time he was bumped off. The artist, he's got an alibi that he was at Miss Plummer's. The noospaper guy, he was to Albee's farm with the secretary. Miss Camford, as they call her, she was to the Country Club with Mr. Getty. Maybe. Maybe not."

"People saw her there," said Maggie, interested in spite of herself.

"Maybe," said the driver. "And maybe people just *think* they seen her. Now, there's been many cases I've heard of where there was a double. She could for instance have a twin sister that was impoisonating her."

"If she'd had a twin sister, it would have come out before this," said Maggie, disappointed.

"That's not necessarily the case," said he. "Those things get hushed up. Now, you take for instance Hitler. He's got a double. Why the people in Goimany, they never see Hitler. They think they do, but all they see is his double. Same with the movie stars. They all got doubles. They never let on that Ardila Nynn was dead for one *year*. They took and put her in a special kind of tomb they got out there in Hollywood, and her double went right on acting in pictures for *one* year."

"I don't believe it," said Maggie.

"You don't have to," said he. "And it would still be true. There's more impoisonating done than you'd ever think. Now take Miss Camford's husband, for instance. *He* could have a double that's impoisonating him, and that could be why she don't know he's dead."

"Who's dead?" asked Maggie.

"Why, her husband, of course," said the driver. "These other newspaper babies knew *that*, all right. One of them said he called up his mother—"

"Whose mother?"

"Why, the husband's mother."

"Mrs. Haverhill?"

"That's it. Mr. Haverhill's mother was who he called up. She is very wealthy, and she says her son died four years ago in Paris."

"No," said Maggie. "It would have been in the newspapers."

"Well, it's going to be in the papers tomorrow, how he died four years ago. But *she* don't know it, see? And I'll tell you why. It's been someone impoisonating him."

"You're sure they said that?"

"Absolutely," said the driver. "The guy that was talking was the one that rung up the mother himself. Very wealthy, she is, and she told him her son was dead and buried four years ago over in Paris. What's more, Captain Hofer said all right, they could print it. Yep! He's been dead four long years now, in Paris."

"Captain Hofer knows that?" Maggie asked. "Captain Hofer said that?"

"Yep," said the driver. "I know him. I knew him when he was just a cop. Just a cop."

"But—hasn't he arrested anybody?"

"Somethin' cookin'," said the driver. "He's got somebody down to the station house right now, grilling them."

"Who?"

"I wouldn't know," he said. "It's only what I hoid."

He turned off now from the main road into the dusty road that ran through the fields. There were lights in the boat-house, looking unbelievably far away in the faint mist that was rising again from the marshes. There was that rank swamp smell again, and that sense of desolate space, no time, nothing.

"It's a lonely place," said the driver. "Nothing but frogs. I got no use for frogs."

He stopped the cab before the house, and reached back to open the door.

"Wait!" said a man's voice. "Who is it?"

"It's me, Mr. Getty," answered Maggie.

"Well, Miss Camford doesn't want to be disturbed just now," he said. "Come back in the morning."

"I live here," said Maggie.

"You can come back in the morning," said Getty, "but Miss Camford doesn't want you now."

"I want to see Miss Dolly, please," said Maggie. "She wants me."

"Not now," he said.

"Well . . . !" said the taxi driver, deeply shocked. "If she lives here, she got a right to go in."

"I want to see Miss Dolly, please," said Maggie doggedly.

It had come into her head that the lighted house was empty. Nobody in it . . . Only Hiram Getty prowling around in the dark.

"I want to see Miss Dolly," she said more loudly.

"I'll tell her then," said Getty, and went up the steps.

"That's Mr. Getty," said the driver in a low and confidential tone. "He lives out over the Point. Very wealthy."

"Is he?" said Maggie. She got out but she stood close to the cab. She liked the driver now, she was glad of his company, very glad.

"All right!" said Getty from the porch. "You can come in."

"Well . . . You'll wait, won't you?" said Maggie to the driver.

"Why, certainly," he said, aggrieved again. "Anyways I haven't got paid yet."

Miss Dolly was in the dining-room sitting at the table under the harsh overhead light that hung from the ceiling.

"Maggie, I'm so glad you came. I was afraid you wouldn't come, Maggie," Miss Dolly said in a sombre monotone. "I thought I'd have to go through this—alone."

Her dark eyes looked past Maggie at nothing; she was very pale and so tense that her rouged lips seemed stretched.

"I've come to the end," she said. "I—"

"Oh, the cab!" cried Maggie. "The taxi's going away!"

She ran to the door and opened it. The cab was driving away through the fields.

"Driver!" she called.

"Stop that!" said Getty. "I paid him—"

"Dri—" she began again, when Getty put his hand over her mouth, a strong, hot smothering hand. She tried to pull it away, and the ridge of hair on the back of it was damp, and she lost consciousness standing on her feet with her eyes open.

But only for the space of a long breath. He took his hand away.

"I'm sorry," he said. "But this—this is serious. We can't have that fellow around."

The tail light of the cab looked blurred and far away in the smoky mist.

"Dolly told me you understood the situation," said Getty. "You must realize . . . We're waiting for the fellow—and he won't come, of course, if he thinks there's anyone around."

"What—fellow?" asked Maggie.

"But—don't you know?" Getty demanded. "That fellow Haverhill."

Waiting for him, were they? With the house brightly lit in the empty fields and the misty marshes; they were waiting for a man dead and buried four years ago, three thousand miles away.

TWENTY-ONE

THE ANCIENT fear stirs readily. In the beginning of things, men in dark forests and on windy plains shook with fear of the dead. They piled great stones on them to keep them still, made chants to soothe the restless spirits, slit living throats to placate those in their graves.

No! Maggie said to herself. I don't believe in things like that. If Mr. Haverhill is dead, they can wait forever and he won't come back.

The tail-light of the taxi twinkled in the haze and vanished, and she was aware of the chorus of insects and the frogs. Well, she said to herself, I am stranded here, after all.

A queer grim resignation began to rise in her. She could not imagine what these two were waiting for, she could not imagine what was going to happen. But she could stand sturdy and undismayed against it, whatever it might be.

She went into the dining-room where Miss Dolly sat smoking with her elbows on the table.

"I feel so cold, Maggie."

"Shall I make you a cup of tea, Miss Dolly? Or coffee?"

"No, thank you, Maggie. I feel so cold—and dreadful."

"That's too bad, Miss Dolly," said Maggie, affably, and sat down across the table.

"Why should anyone want to harm *me*, Maggie? All I want—all I've *ever* wanted, Maggie, was to be let alone, to be happy in my own way."

"Well, that's quite a lot to want, it seems to me," said Maggie.

For the relation between them was wholly changed now. Miss Dolly no longer seemed the sophisticated woman of the world; Maggie no longer felt like the ambitious and eager young creature who could learn so much from her. It seemed to her that Miss Dolly was lost and drifting, and that she herself had found her feet.

"It seems to me so little Maggie. I never *wanted* to hurt anyone."

Well, you have hurt people. People much better than yourself.

"You don't think I'm horrible, do you, Maggie?"

I don't know what I think of you. Only if there wasn't something bad in you, something very bad, you couldn't look like this. So pale and desperate. So—guilty.

"Maggie, can't you say anything?"

"I'm trying to think things out, Miss Dolly."

"Maggie, if I heard him coming . . . Maggie, I don't know how I can stand it."

"Hear who coming, Miss Dolly?"

"My husband."

"You won't hear him, Miss Dolly."

"But he said he'd come."

"Miss Dolly," said Maggie. "He's dead and buried."

There was a silence between them. The full tide, flowing in, lapped against the walls, and hearing that you had to think of the creek that ran through the marshes to the sea.

"I wanted you with me, Maggie," said Miss Dolly. "You can see that I'm just sitting here waiting—in dread."

"You mean I'm a witness?" said Maggie. "Who is it you're waiting for, Miss Dolly?"

"I told you."

"And why is Mr. Getty here, Miss Dolly?"

"Because he's my friend. Because he's kind to me. Kinder than *you*."

Someone moved past the lighted window. It's only Mr. Getty, Maggie told herself. He's waiting out there—for somebody. The lapping of the water seemed very loud, the rowboat was bumping against the wall.

"Miss Dolly," said Maggie, "let's go upstairs."

Because someone was trying to open the back door with a key, and that wouldn't be Mr. Getty. That must be—someone else.

"Maggie!" said Miss Dolly, in a whisper. "Maggie, do you hear?"

"Yes, I do. Come upstairs, Miss Dolly."

Dolly sat rigid in her chair. Maggie rose and took her hand and tried to draw her to her feet. Then a shot came, frightfully loud, echoing and trembling in the air. Maggie's hand flew to her heart that seemed to check as if the sound had struck it.

"Hiram's killed him. . . ." said Miss Dolly, faintly, and her breast rose in a long sigh.

It was a sigh of relief; the look of terror had gone from her eyes.

"You meant this to happen!" Maggie cried. That was plain to her now. That was what Hiram Getty was here for, to kill someone. "*Who is it?*"

"It's all over now," said Miss Dolly.

There was the sound of a key in the lock again, and they both faced the swing door. The back door had opened now, footsteps were crossing the kitchen. The swing door was pushing open. Miss Dolly gave a scream; she rose and rushed towards the stairs; she ran up them, stumbling.

It was Johnny Cassidy, with a streak of blood across his mouth and a gun in his hand.

"Oh, you're here?" he said, casually.

Maggie could not speak. He looked, she thought, like a wild beast just come from the kill. As he approached her, she backed away from him.

"What's—happened?" she said.

"Funny things," he said, and drew his hand across his

forehead, leaving a streak of blood there. "Getty shot at me, and I jumped him and took away his gun."

"Did you—"

"Did I kill him?" said Johnny. "No. He's out, but he isn't dead. Now I want to see Dolly."

That must not happen. If only somebody would come. . . . If only Captain Hofer would come. . . .

"She did this, you know," said Johnny. "She gave me the key to the back door this morning and she told me to come back at ten-thirty. She said she'd arrange to be alone. She said she'd have eight hundred dollars for me, so that I could get away. Then she must have had some fine tale for Getty. She must have told him to shoot anyone he saw trying to come in by the back door. Maybe he knew who I was; maybe he didn't. Anyhow, it didn't work right. None of her plans have worked right. She's finished now."

"You mustn't blame her for what Mr. Getty did . . ."

"Mr. Getty did as he was told," said Johnny, in the same casual, offhand tone. "I know she wanted to get rid of me. She had to. But I didn't think she'd try this. It isn't like her. She's not usually so direct. Do you know, I can find it in my heart—to be sorry she did this."

"Yes," said Maggie, seizing on this. "She didn't mean this—"

"Oh, she meant it all right," he said. "For years and years she's wanted to get rid of me. I've wanted to get free from her, too. But we never could. There was a bond between us— the damnedest bond. . . . I've been blackmailing her for years, off and on. You wouldn't think *that* would make a bond, would you? But it did. When I was broke, or in trouble, I'd make her give me money. But, by God, when she needed money, she didn't mind asking me for it. And I'd give it to her—if I had any. Queer situation . . . Maybe we hated each other. But we've had some damn good times together, here, and in Paris. We've laughed together a lot."

There was one clear idea in Maggie's mind, to keep him from going up those stairs. He was quiet enough, almost mild; but it was the quiet of someone who had come to the very end. Why didn't somebody come . . . ?

"Johnny," she said, "she hasn't done anything—"

He smiled.

"You're right," he said. "You couldn't have put it better. She hasn't done anything. She's *never* done anything. She's never hated anyone and never loved anyone. She's the supreme catalyst. She causes things to happen and then shuts

151

her eyes. She never had a husband, you know, never had a lover. She couldn't care that much for anyone. She'd lead a man on, and then she'd run away from him, in a panic. That's what she'd have done with Getty."

He sat down on the table, holding the gun loosely in his hand.

"You've got blood on your face," said Maggie. "I'll get a towel—"

"Stay where you are," he said. "It's too bad she got you into this, you poor little kid. Take it easy now. You can't stop what's going to happen. You've been in all of it, haven't you? Even the Angel episode. That was pure accident, you know. He had some sort of stroke and he fell through the rotten railing and landed in the rowboat, pretty hard. But he wasn't dead. She didn't kill him. All she did was to let him die there. She even cried, sitting inside the house with me. He was a killjoy, come here to spoil her fun."

He looked down at the gun and Maggie looked too. Blood was running along his thin hand and dripping on to the floor.

"You're hurt," she said. "Let me tie up your arm."

"It doesn't matter," he said. "She didn't kill her uncle, either. Not she! She only whispered to me that if somebody didn't stop him, he'd take away the last bit of money she had, or ever would have. Of course, she did know I happened to need money badly, very badly just then. She did happen to mention that he was leaving her something handsome in his will—if he didn't alter it. She just said she'd leave him alone in the house, and maybe I'd come back—and see if I couldn't plead with him. And I came back."

"You . . . ?"

"Me," he said. "It was a bad thing to do. I didn't have *that* clear in my mind when I left you at Mrs. Albee's. I had some fine schemes for persuading him to let Dolly keep her money. Fine schemes. I've talked a good many people into a good many things. But I don't know. Maybe I knew all the time what it would lead to."

"While we—were there . . . ?"

"Right while we were together," he said. "But it was a lovely day. You're such a good little kid, and I felt good myself. But he played into my hands. I don't think I'd have been able to walk up to him and smash him on the head with a stick. It's easier than you'd think to kill someone who's running away from you, or someone who's attacking you. But in cold blood, as they say . . ."

He took a cigarette out of his pocket; he looked at it and put it back.

"But he started right in at me. You, sir, I've heard of you, sir. A common swindler, sir. Leave this house, sir. So I stopped having cold blood, and I could do it. I tied some stones to his arms and I thought he'd stay put. But I evidently didn't do it the right way. He came out. And then Dolly lost her head. If she'd shut up, there needn't have been much trouble. I'd sent that telegram, saying he was going to Boston. Nobody could prove anything. I was arrested in Spain by the Franco outfit, and I talked myself out of that. I've been arrested other times, and I got out of it. But the great stark fact of death was too much for Dolly. She panicked. First she tried to put it all off on Neely—which was childish. He didn't have anything to do with anything. Then she thought up this husband, and that made things worse."

He rose.

"Where—are you going?" Maggie asked.

"Upstairs," he said. "To get that eight hundred dollars. Don't you think I've earned it?"

"Don't," she said. "Please don't. I'll go up and get the money for you."

"No," he said. "It's too late, Maggie."

"You can—get away."

"Not now," he said. "It's too late. This is the payoff, Maggie."

"Please!" she said. "You can't go up like that—with blood on your face. Please . . . I'll help you to get away—"

He was moving toward the stairs.

"Miss Dolly!" she called with all her might. "Miss Dolly, lock your door!"

"That won't help," said Johnny.

"Dolly! Dolly!" she cried. But there was no answer and no sound from overhead.

"She's probably taken some of her little pills," said Johnny. "That's another way she has to escape annoyance."

Maggie ran in front of him and spread out her arms.

"Stop! Oh, stop! Think what you're doing—"

"I'm sorry about you," he said. "I could have been very fond of you—ten years ago."

He put her aside and started up the stairs. Everything vital and quick and strong in her fused into one passionate resolution. He was going slowly, with one hand on the rail; she

153

stooped and darted under his arm and ran frantically up the stairs ahead of him. She was too breathless to call again; she ran through the big room to the bedroom; the door was open and the light was on, and Miss Dolly lay in bed with her eyes closed.

"Miss Dolly . . ." said Maggie, in a faint, breathless voice. "Wake up! Wake up!"

Miss Dolly's shoulder as she grasped it was warm and smooth; she was breathing. But she did not open her eyes. And Johnny Cassidy was coming through the other room.

"Wake up!" said Maggie and scratched that smooth shoulder.

"Don't . . . !" Dolly murmured, fretfully, and opened her eyes.

"Wake up! Johnny's here!"

"Johnny's here," he repeated from the doorway.

Her eyes were wide wide open now; she lay flat on her pillow, looking up at him.

"Go away, Maggie," he said.

"No," said Maggie.

She sat down, suddenly, and heavily, on the bed and stretched her arm across Miss Dolly.

"You'll have to go," said Johnny.

Miss Dolly said nothing and did not stir.

He took Maggie's wrist and pulled her to her feet. She tried to hang back but he slung her around behind him; he pushed her out into the big room and closed the door. She opened it.

"No!" she said, in a hoarse loud voice. She was not afraid of Johnny Cassidy, not afraid for herself. There was nothing left in her but that one clear fierce passion to defend the woman lying there.

"Look here! Get out!" said Johnny.

"No!"

He looked at her, a look almost sorrowful.

"Like a damn little Scotch terrier," he said. "But you've got to get out."

"No!" she cried, in a shout. "Miss Dolly, get up! He'll kill you!"

"Maggie . . ." came Miss Dolly's voice in a faint wail.

Maggie tried to rush past him but he stopped her. He threw the gun down on the couch and picked her up and carried her out on the balcony. She struggled desperately and silently, but he moved his shoulders, swinging her a little like a bundle, and he threw her off, down into that water.

TWENTY-TWO

It was cold as death, closing over her head. But she came up at once and began to swim automatically. Her hand struck against the rowboat and she held to that for a moment. Then she edged hand over hand to the ramp and crawled up it on her hands and knees. Then she had to rest.

She was crying and sobbing, lying on the damp salty grass. She was crying because she could not get up. She tried, but she could not remember how to move her feet and her wet skirts twisted around her. She was defeated now.

A car was coming; a great blinding light shone on her as she raised her head. She heard a shot.

"Help!" she called. But she was not sure if she made any sound. She got up on her knees, with a dreadful effort.

"Maggie?" said Neely's voice. "Is that you?"

"Miss Dolly!" she said. "Go in quick—and see—"

"Hofer and the others are in the house," he said. "What are you doing here?"

He laid his hand on her head. "You're wet," he said. "Soaking." He helped her to her feet and put his arm around her. "Better come into the house," he said.

She wanted to go in there, she had to go in there. Two cars were standing before the house and there was a man standing on the porch.

"Who's this?" he asked.

"She lives here," said Neely, and the man let them pass.

There was nobody there. The lights were on, very bright, and there were footsteps overhead.

"I want to go upstairs," she said.

"They wouldn't let you," he said. "Here—"

He took the cover off the couch in the dining-room and wrapped it around her. "Sit down," he said, "and I'll get you a drink of whiskey."

"No . . ." she said, her teeth chattering. "N-never . . ."

"Then I'll make you some coffee," he said.

He pushed her into the shabby armchair and went into the kitchen; he was back again in a moment.

"Why are you so wet?" he asked. He had a dish towel in his hand and he began to dry her hair.

"Don't—bother . . ." she said.

The boards overhead creaked under a heavy tread.

"Please find out . . ." she said. "Please—right away."

"All right!" he said, and went running lightly up the stairs.

He was gone so long and she was so cold. The couch-cover was wet now, and it was dirty; a moldy smell came from it. She took it off and stood up as Neely came down the stairs again.

"It's all over," he said. "Don't worry any more."

"What—?" she said. "What—happened?"

"Both dead," said Neely. "You'd better sit down again. You look quite sick and funny."

"How—dead?" she asked.

"Johnny shot himself," said Neely. "Only first he smothered her with a pillow."

"Othello!" she cried.

He pushed her down into the chair again. "I wish there was a blanket," he said. "And your shoes—"

"Look here!" she said, trying to steady her voice. "Don't you—*care*—one bit?"

He shook his head.

"You don't care—about Miss Dolly being—murdered?"

"No. Why should I? At first I liked her, but I stopped. She got me locked up in jail. She made a big fool of me."

She leaned her head against the back of the chair and looked up at him.

"You're just not human!" she said.

"What's the matter with you?" he asked, angrily. "You told me that before. What have I done that's so wrong? Nothing at all. I work very hard and I mind my own business. I don't drink—"

"You don't?"

"No, never. I don't tell lies, either. Yet it's always me you go for. I'm the one that's not human. And why?" He spoke with a sort of severe wonder. "Because I put a dead old man in the water? Because I don't shed crocodile tears for those two upstairs? I'd like to know what I've done you think is so bad."

"I don't know," she said.

Maybe Neely is good. And Johnny was bad—so bad. . . . Maybe I'm unjust—and mean. Maybe I'm a hypocrite, Maggie thought, with tears running down her face. Maybe I don't know *anything*—about human nature. . . .

"Here," said Neely. "Here's a present I bought for you. Now I'm going away."

He tossed a little box into her lap and went out into the hall; the front door closed after him. She waited a moment and then she took off the lid. There was a wrist-watch there, quite a nice little silver watch.

Oh, dear! she cried to herself. Oh, dear . . . !

"Now!" said Captain Hofer, grimly. "Now, then young lady, what have you got to say for yourself?"

He was angry at her; perhaps he suspected her of all sorts of things. He had a right to be angry; she had not co-operated with him.

"I don't know . . ." she said.

"You're all dripping wet," he said, with a scowl on his scarlet face. "What's happened to you?"

"I—don't know . . ." she said again. That was so silly, but she couldn't help it.

"This won't do," he said. "No use your getting pneumonia. Come along now. I'll take you back to Mrs. Mayfield at the hotel and you can have a hot bath and get to bed. You can talk tomorrow."

"And Mr. Getty?" she asked.

"He'll be all right," said Captain Hofer.

He wasn't angry or mean. He was kind. Oh, dear! Oh, dear! How could you ever figure things out?

"Come now," he said. "Don't take this so hard. You're young and you'll get over it." He pursed his lips and shook his head. "Very young," he said.